Devoid

of

Shelter

Hypocrisy & Reality

Book:4

fiction

by

'Videh' Arvind Kumar

1967 to 1968

(a novel)

(class 5th)

(Naglaa-Kath, Kunwarpur)

Dedication

Devoid of Shelter
(Hypocrisy & Reality:
Book 4)

Dedicated to my maternal relatives - my Naanaa, Naanee, Maamaa, Maamee, maternal cousins and all the affectionate ones there - who took me under their shelter and refuge, lest I should have been a wretch today!

Table of Contents

Copyright

Devoid of Shelter
(Hypocrisy & Reality:
Book 4)
First published in July, 2024
All rights reserved
@ *'Videh' Arvind Kumar*
Lucknow, India

The right of *'Videh' Arvind Kumar* to be identified as author and publisher of this work has been asserted in accordance with the Copyright, Design and Patents Act.

This is a work of fiction. The names and characters and events portrayed in this book are fictitious and the product of the author's imagination and any resemblance or similarity to real or actual persons, living or dead, is entirely coincidental and not intended by the author or publisher.

Preface

'Devoid of Shelter', the fourth volume in the fiction series 'Hypocrisy & Reality' furthers the journey of the protagonist into the world where he discovered to his dismay that he had no place on the globe which he could call as his home; he had no place of his own where he could take shelter during the day, and during the night. He somehow makes do with seeking shelter with the relatives – maternal chiefly; not as a transitory phenomenon, but for good, until he himself took command of his life, snatching himself away from the indolent lifestyle of his parents. He also discovered during the refuge that however meritorious one might be, without the good base of ancestry, one is not considered as such. *Rotee, Kapdaa* and *Makaan* are said to be the quintessence of life, of which, none was affordable to the protagonist during the regime of one's parents.

गृहस्थ के धर्म:- महाभारत उद्योग पर्व

पृथिव्याम् सागरान्तायाम् द्वाविमौ पुरुषाधमौ।

गृहस्थश्च निरारम्भ: सारम्भश्चैव भिक्षुक: ॥

(समुद्र पर्यन्त इस सारी पृथ्वी में ये दो प्रकार के अधम पुरुष है:- अकर्मण्य गृहस्थ, और कर्मों में लगा हुआ सन्यासी।)

द्वावेव न विराजेते विपरीतेन कर्मणा।

गृहस्थश्च निरारम्भ: कार्यवांश्चैव भिक्षुक: ॥

(दो ही अपने विपरीत कर्म के कारण शोभा नहीं पाते:- अकर्मण्य गृहस्थ, और प्रपञ्चों में लगा हुआ सन्यासी।)

महाभारत: सम्भव पर्व, शकुन्तलोपाख्यान, कण्व ऋषि उवाच)

नारीणाम् चिरवासो हि बान्धवेषु न रोचते।

कीर्तिचारित्रधर्मघ्नस्तस्मान्नयत मा चिरम्॥

(स्त्रियों का अपने भाई-बन्धुओं के यहाँ अधिक दिनों तक रहना अच्छा नहीं होता; वह उनकी कीर्ति, शील तथा पातिव्रत्य धर्म का नाश करने वाला होता है। अत: इसे अविलम्ब पति के घर पहुँचा दो!)

'Videh' Arvind Kumar
Aashrum, Lucknow, UP, India
July, 2024

Transcripts of *Hindee* letters and *maatraas*

Keeping in view the special pronunciations of *Sanskrit* words, and with a view to differentiating between the disparate pronunciations, we have followed the following regimen of transcription from *Devnaagaree* to Roman script. This clarification will help the readers appreciate the nuances of linguistic specificities and enjoy the text in truly desired sense. Moreover, the vernacular words, particularly nouns, have been italicized.

अ a, आ aa, इ i, ई ee, उ u, ऊ oo, ऋ ri, ए e, ऐ ai, ओ o, औ ऑ au, अं an, अः :,
क ka, का kaa, कि ki, की kee, कु ku, कू koo, कृ kri, के ke, कै kai, को ko, कौ kau, कं kan, कः kah;

1. Come Rains And Crumbles Our Shelter

Enter Mother

After the fourth standard exams of my son having been over, as usual, I had been parcelled by my indolent husband with my son and the daughter – the only two issues with me by that time – off to my parent's house. Irrespective of whether they liked it or not, my husband assumed that this was incumbent upon my parents to take care of his family during leisure time. I too felt comfortable and at ease while at my parents' house, for at my husband's house, I got constantly tortured at the latter's hands, although there was no little torture at parent's house as well where I had to do manual chores in agricultural fields including the cutting of fodder for the cattle. Nonetheless, while with my husband, there wasn't a single day or night when he did not create ruckus on this or that imaginary pretext. My husband was a fiend in his earlier life in fact and the tendencies of his earlier life could not forsake him, or it could be said, that he could not shake off his *sanskaars* of his previous birth or births. Everybody in the area knew this fact, but nobody expressed it openly before him. And expediently so! My husband behaved also as if he were a permanent creature – to live on this planet or in this house, more so, with us, for time immemorial; therefore feeling at liberty to behave in howsoever or whatsoever cruel and sinful a manner!

I was having the inkling that he had been eased out of the teaching job at the town given his tantrums and irrational behaviour with the faculty there. How could he behave rationally in his teaching job at school whereas he had never behaved in a civilized manner at his home, his household! Sitting at home, while having food beside the fireplace, he looked like a dreaded beast, feared by one and all including not only the kids – his innocent issues – but also, the family elders, his father included. Now in hindsight, I realise that he was prone to having intoxicants – the liquor, tobacco and drugs – and he behaved bestially under the influence of those poisons, the intoxicants. On top of that, his brain had already cracked in the wake of excessive wailing at the time of the death of his young mother, as he had already divulged to us in the millet field!

Everything was going on smoothly in my father's village and we were approaching the end of June that year - 1967, with the plans to leave for our husband's village in the first week of July when the schools were to open. My son was studying in the town school there, and we were supposed to reach there by that time.

At that time, however, did strike me the doubly sad news. The news arrived from my in-laws' side that our portion of house - whatever it was – had collapsed in rains with a thud. I feared for my belongings – whatever meagre we had in that name - for everything whatsoever was under that shared piece of roof only. I was, however, apprised that before the coming down of the roof and sensing the impending and oncoming catastrophe or calamity, all the household items of ours had been shifted to the portion of our elder aunt – to the smaller arm of U – by our *Nanad* – the younger sister of my father. I could visualise the gory scene of the mud and thatch habitat when its roof would have collapsed with a thud leaving everything in the open – under open sky, and letting the torrents splash down heavily inside the room flooding everything in the length and breadth of the shared room – now shared by only two of us, my husband's family and the family of his elder brother.

My heart sank: where would we live now? That was a sad news for all of us elders at my parents' side. But not for my son – the only male child I had by then. He came running to me – having been informed by his playmates that our habitat had collapsed – and asked me gleefully, "*Beebee*! Has our house collapsed?" He did apparently not fathom the import of his words and the incongruity of his smile with whatever he was conveying. I took pity on him: how ignorant he was! About his impending fate! He did not realise the calamity that was to beset us in near future and thereafter, given the absolute worthlessness of his father. My son thought that as the old house had collapsed, a new one would automatically come up or be constructed – possibly like *Badee Ammaa's* one; alike the emergence of a sphinx from the ashes! But *Badee Ammaa's* son was duly employed and earning money, sanely. My kid did not yet know what sort of a resourceless, skill-less as well as skull-less his father was! And that his father wasn't earning anything, rather, he was squandering whatever money I got from my parents, so to say, as parsimony. It was never to be – the construction of collapsed house! Unlike a sphinx – rising from the ruins! I knew his father could never raise a new house or even think of it; he lacked that faculty totally – the resourcefulness and the imagination. He was a madcap in fact; how could he manage such things – things of household importance: the *Rotee, Kapdaa* and *Makaan*, the quintessence of life, the compulsory conditions for living on this planet. A household management is the most challenging task in the universe. His father was not even able to manage a B. Ed. degree for being eligible for teaching the students at school, how could he run a household? I sometimes wonder how the family elders could even think of arranging a marriage for such an unworthy and insane lad!

My son asked me, "But we shall get another house!"

I became all the more morose.

Not only this shattering news, the accompanying news came in: that *Badee Ammaa* had died. *Badee Ammaa!* She was my saviour! She used to save me from the ever-existent tyranny of my deranged husband. To only some extent though! After her house having been parted rearward, though that protection was no more available, still her presence in the world – on this planet – beyond the brick wall, was a sort of consolation and assurance for me in that there was someone who could be approached with a petition against my mad man. Now that shield, too, had vanished, as though, all at once.

Both the shelters – the *homestead* and the person of *Badee Ammaa* - had been shattered simultaneously, as though the Providence had as though dispensed to render us shelter-less in all the respects! As though the Providence had pre-decided to rule against us,

and to make us devoid of a roof over our heads for good! In the changed circumstances, we now owned no roof over our heads to call the same as our own!

Badee Ammaa in fact did not die all of a sudden or unexpectedly. She was at the time of her death living with her son's family at the latter's place of employment at *Ajmer*. *Ammaa* had suffered a paralytic stroke last session – when my son was in fourth standard. She lived alone in her secluded house at that juncture. She had little contact with the family members in the *Baakhar*. However, her younger brothers-in-law used to call her or hearken her once in a while from far off while rearing the cattle or shifting the cattle from the yard to the open space, and if there was a remorseless as well as mirthful repartee from *Badee Ammaa* – for which she was famous (or infamous!?) – her junior relatives felt assured that everything was OK. That was almost a daily chore. One fine morning, however, it so happened that *Badee Ammaa* did not respond in her usual virile style as was her wont. Her brother-in-law, *Mukhiyaa,* on not being responded spontaneously sensed something odd, something untoward having happened with his elder sister-in-law. And indeed it had! She had suffered a paralytic stroke, losing her speech. A mayhem ensued all around following that mishap: the eldest member and the most influential member of the family had collapsed, allegorically, as though *Bheeshm Pitaamah* had collapsed in the proverbial *Mahaabhaarata Yuddha. Badee Ammaa* had collapsed in the war of life! *Mukhiyaajee* repeated his complaint that it was already suggested at the time of constructing this house rearwards, that is, facing the rear side of the *Baakhar,* that the old lady must not be left to remain in the seclusion, for old ones are susceptible to any kind of uncertainties at any time. He also added that had he not contemplated venturing to enquire further – on not getting a response from the old lady - the old lady would have died on the spot itself. That was a lesson in old age living style indeed! For those who forsake their parents to remain alone, at the hands of Providence!

Mukhiyaajee also complained, though in light vein, that his *Bhaabhee* – wife of his elder brother - never uttered God's name even by mistake; that she was such an atheist! He also cracked a joke on her by telling a parable: once a lady alike her lived somewhere who also never uttered God's name. When she was about to die, the kindly people thought of making her utter God's name so that she could attain *Moksha* – salvation - and they brought a plough – *Hal,* or *Har* in rural

parlance – before her eyes. And lo, instead of saying who had brought the *'Har'* or *'Hari',* the old lady demanded: 'who has brought this wooden log here?' To everybody's consternation coupled with suppressed laughter and chuckle! Thus jeopardising finally her chances of attaining *Param Gati!* The *Moksha!* The *Nibbaan!*

Ammaa was taken by her son along with him to the city of his employment for recuperation and treatment. But who has ever recovered from the paralytic stroke? The stroke of impending death! After living for a few months she ultimately succumbed to her incapacitated condition and died. And that day was the day about which we received this shattering news from that city at our father's home!

For me, the hapless one, the day was a devastating one, shattering one! Having received a double dose of sad news!

XXX

2. Where To Go In The Next Session

Enter Mother

Having blocked all the roads for return for us the Providence presented two posers before me: where to go after a week when we were planning to leave for our home – in-law's home? And, where to school my son who was so gifted

10

and brilliant?

However, I had a very considerate and affectionate maternal side fortunately as if a recompense for my ill-luck on in-law's side. They were exceptionally kind and considerate and sympathetic towards their girl – a wretched girl – whose marriage they had solemnised with a dud. And were paying heavily for that oversight. My sisters-in-law, that is, the wives of my two brothers were all sympathetic towards me and anxious about the gloomy fate ahead I was poised for in the given circumstances.

The comments of my elder brother – who was so ferocious and cruel-hearted otherwise – were like this: 'Do not worry, sister, we shall take care of you and your issues – son and girl – whom we shall get admitted to the school of the hamlet nearby, that is, *Naglaa Kath*. He may continue his studies there unhindered and carefreely....' *blah blah*. Hearing this, coming as it did from the mouth of my elder brother while having his supper at home sitting beside the wall of the kitchen – he always sat like that while taking his meals – I felt like my anxiety getting evaporated to some extent, yet a lingering feeling of despondency was ever looming at the level of my subconscious mind. However, my son got very happy to hear of it, for he never liked to go to

his father's home: for that was like a jail for him, for there was no freedom like it was available at my parents' house; there was no greenery around, nor the affability in the demeanours of the inhabitants as it was available at my parents' village and family. The idea that he would stay throughout the year at his maternal grandparents' house filled my son with extraordinary mirth and pleasure as if getting rid of the claustrophobic company of his father was the source of happiness and aim of life for him. And indeed it was as such for me, too; I also thought almost on those lines albeit subconsciously, if only not overtly. After all, I had to contend with that wretched existence only in the end – that of living with my husband, in those wretched conditions!

Nonetheless, it was necessary to visit the habitat at least for once for salvaging and recovering whatever articles were obtaining at my husband's house in the name of possessions or belongings.

On the appointed day when we were scheduled to make a departure for an academic year ahead for my son to my husband's habitat, we made a trip this time, temporarily only – only to return immediately. I packed a few articles in my handbag and along with my teenager son and lap-laden daughter accompanied by my nephew – the son of my younger brother – I undertook a short trip to the village of my husband. I was sure, nothing would be available there, for my husband had already left for his aunt's *(buaa's)* village for taking up a teaching job – *ad hoc* one - in the school there that was running under the patronage of his *foofaa* – the husband of his aunt *(buaa)*. We reached the village almost unbidden and unwelcome: who would welcome the family of an indolent and worthless fellow who could not manage even the home for one's family, what to speak of food and clothing. The *Badee Ammaa* – my godmother – had already gone to her heavenly abode – or to another existence on this planet, who knows (?) – so the only creatures now residing in that spiritless small shanty were the younger sister of my husband and the sister-in-law of my husband, that is, the wife of his elder brother. The *Baakhar* had already been sequestered, i.e. divided into three parts, our one being only a quarter of the whole. So even if the happiness that was generated due to augmented privacy in the new circumstances was simultaneously nullified by the claustrophobic atmosphere owing to the presence of my ever antagonistic sister-in-law, that is, the wife of my husband's elder brother, and the suffocating spectacle of lofty walls that had come up, of late, in the erstwhile

sprawling *Baakhar*. It was no more a *Baakhar* now, no more a sprawling common residential area that was earlier meant for womenfolk of the family! It resembled more truly a confinement, a jail – a benign one although!

My husband was absent. We were to fend for ourselves in his absence, with our part of the habitat already having collapsed, and with no arrangement for stay and food etc. in the collapsed and run-down circumstances. We were at the sweet mercy of the wife of my husband's elder brother.

The younger sister of my husband who was simply a teenager, an adolescent, at that time showed goodwill and sympathy and pleasure at our arrival, however. Nonetheless, she had little say in anything in the household, she herself being a motherless child and at present at the mercy of her elder sister-in-law, that is, the wife of her elder brother. Her necessaries of life were being taken care of by her elder brother only, for my husband was incapable of affording any responsibilities of anybody in the house. How could he; he was unable to take the responsibility of even his own close family – his wife and two kids! How could he afford to provide food and shelter to his younger sister and his father?

My nephew who was accompanying me on this short trip

felt depressed at the sight of this pathetic condition on the ground of his *Buaa*'s home when he saw – even as I myself saw – the gaping hole in the roof of the *kutcha* hall which was till a few months back taken as our home – sweet home. Juxtaposing that situation with the pleasurable and comfortable conditions of my parents I felt utterly depressed at the prospect of my future life, for I knew that my indolent and duffer husband would never ever be able to acquire or build a nest for his family which he had been procreating so mindlessly without any concern for arranging for them the food, clothing and housing – *Rotee, kapdaa and makaan.*

I arranged all the articles of my establishment in a sack or so and kept those in the portion of my sister-in-law. And declared that we meant to leave immediately. I had not let my nephew leave who was desperate to get rid of this hell of a habitat immediately, unaccustomed as he was to such pathetic situations of households. His own living conditions were befitting those of princes and princesses in a sense! I told him that we would return together, for we should not stay back more than a day or two there, for there were no provisions and necessaries available there for maintaining one's existence even for a day. That was a figurative comment on the worth of my man –

the husband, who was given me camouflaged as the best educated guy in the area! The solo BA!

The younger sister of my husband was expecting that we had come for stay or at least for stay for some weeks, but when we disclosed that we were leaving the next day, she became morose, my sister-in-law, the spouse of my husband's elder brother, of course, showing signs of relief on her face at this decision of mine.

In a dejected mood we returned from that hell of a residence and heaved a sigh of relief when we boarded the train to my parent's village. Shelterless even though we had been rendered decidedly!

XXX

3. Father's Reliance On Nepotism

Enter Father

In the millet field where we were weeding, my son asked me, 'Tell us something about your *Veerpuraa* stint; why you were shunted out of that school too, and what the mystery behind the particular lady – the wife of the Principal of that school visiting the village every year or off and on and seeing you for demanding her one hundred rupees and creating scene in the entire village. Why didn't you pay off those hundred rupees which were their legitimate due? …..That was such a sordid episode, and that continued for almost a decade!...'

When he stopped his harangue, I started narrating thus:

"Post the gory episode of manhandling of the PT teacher at the hands of students of the High School I taught in, and the finger of suspicion having been pointed towards me, given multifarious links of mine with the naughty or bully boys, so to say, I was rusticated from the school by the Management: on the pretext that I was not qualified for teaching at schools, for I did not possess a B. Ed. degree. What to do next was the big question; however, I was least perturbed. That was not my wont. There were so many others in the family to take care of me; and of such other concerns as my share of landholding. At least I had that type of notion even if not the others might be having that notion.

And indeed they cared. I received a missive from one of my worthy uncles – a person with old world clout – from the village *Somnaa* where he hailed from. He sent the message that at the school of *Veerpuraa* I could be taken in temporary employ of the school for teaching English there. In fact, in a sense, English has ever been a bread earner for our family. My father being a plucked Matriculate of British era, he had gathered enough English knowledge for being considered a prodigy of English in the preponderantly illiterate rural area: *andhon mein kaanaa raajaa* (in the land of the blind, the one-eyed man is the king!). I immediately grabbed the offer; of course, without taking into cognizance the fact that for such meagre wages – I was paid only one hundred rupees per month by the management -- to sustain one's living at a far off village was tantamount to earning nothing, not to talk of saving something for the family – my wife and son and daughter. I was weak at mathematics as well as arithmetic, resultantly, such *faux pas* was bound to occur. How could I weigh all the *pros and cons* of the proposal?

It was in the year 1967 in the month of July that I set off for my new found job at a remote place from my mother land and reached the abode of my uncle – the husband of my father's sister. This was a few days prior to the visit of my wife and family to my collapsed hut at my village. Till then I was little aware of the ramifications of such stays with the relatives; in my notions I thought that the relatives had a lien over the hospitality of other relatives irrespective of the latter's reluctance. Who would like to spend money on freeloaders? A single person's expenses amount to quite a high sum when occasioned to bear upon others. It's only one's own blood relations whose expenses we bear without making any fuss or having any inhibitions about. When it comes to others than near and dear ones, it assumes the attributes of a burden. The hospitality we show towards a guest is meant for only a day or two. When it goes beyond that the guest is taken to be a stranger and is meted out the same treatment as a stranger would.

I was very happy in the beginning enjoying the privileges of a guest for a few weeks at my aunt's as well as uncle's sprawling abode, but when it came to the end of month and my aunt – the sister of my father – sensed that I would be getting wages in the first week of the month, she started demanding money on this pretext or that. How could I refuse? After all I was obligated to them; I was having free food and lodging with them, and also, nonchalantly inconveniencing them by my presence. Within no time I became an unwelcome persona, a *persona non grata,* in the house of my aunt and uncle.

In fact whether I deserved the job or not is also dubious, for my job was grabbed by me through the workings of nepotism by my uncle, rather, through favouritism – an evil, a social one. That was an additional obligation on me from their side. Soon I came to realise that the decision to have come at this far off village for earning livelihood was naught, that it was merely a *faux pas* on my part. In social relations quite often people do tend to offer phony proposals which are in fact not meant for grabbing; such ornamental offers are meant for only goodwill generation on both the sides: one side has to offer in a perfunctory manner and the other side is supposed to refuse, sensibly, that's all.

Since I was a parasite in the aunt's house, as also, since I was an *ad hoc* teacher thrust upon the school: thrust by way of the clout of my uncle, not by virtue of my qualifications, there was lot of ill-will harboured by personnel towards me at the school as well. Nepotism and favouritism have never been looked upon as virtues by the society, however, pretentious they might try to feign that they liked the one. At the level of the soul, this unrighteousness pinches and nags all the time, and ultimately penalises in worldly terms, too.

With this meagre sum of Rs.100/- a month, I was never able to send any money to my wife and issues that were parked at and burdened on my in-laws for a year. The schools in those days were private affairs and the monetary management of the same was dependent on the collection of fees from the students. Those were called 'unaided schools'. Those schools which got aid from the Govt were called 'aided schools' and the condition of such schools as regards payment of wages to the teachers regularly was a bit better. The unaided teachers seldom got their wages fully or timely or regularly.

One more fact worth bringing to the attention of the reader is that this aid provided by the Govt was an added attraction for people or management to open schools on their landed properties so that they could get a regular source of income for their families. They never paid the full amount of salary to the teachers for which they got the receipt from the teachers, and the sum paid to the teachers was sometimes ridiculously meagre as compared to what they were collecting from the Govt in the name of wages paid to the teachers. This was in fact a hangover of the feudal landlordism that had only recently been abolished by the newly enthroned Govt of independent India, and some feudal lords were desperate to create something to fill that void. And schools were a novel invention to foot the bill. Instead of concentrating on teaching, the management and the teachers were more interested in discussing all the time about the prospects of the school getting the status of an 'Aided' one. This word 'Aided' when added to a school gave the latter a glorious glitter and that was like a hen laying golden eggs for the management of the school; and managements were nothing but certain families, the family fiefdoms.

Even before the idea of family fiefdoms developed in polity, the concept had already taken roots in the form of management of schools. It is surprising to see that the politicians propagating such family fiefdoms unabashedly are also, coincidentally, those sprung up from such schools only. Those teachers and managers in due course flourished as politicians and they created their own political parties which were nothing but their family fiefdoms only with all the posts going to their own blood relations. All privileges reserved for their own family relations and progenies! A travesty of 'democracy'!

"Thus the history of family politicians has traversed through such schools!", my son averred and sighed.

"Indeed! That's so." I affirmed.

Not only now, it has always been like that in all the epochs and ages. During the *Dev Sanskriti* (culture of adoration of gods), particularly, in the east-Asian countries beyond *Burmaa,* initially, there were common people, righteous folks inhabiting those lands, islands and archipelagos; and living peacefully as well as in an egalitarian social system. Gradually, under the influence of human tendency of 'me and mine' the feudal tendencies evolved, and soon those were transformed into family fiefdoms, ultimately degenerating into kingdoms and monarchies and even draconian dictatorships and despotisms. The same has been happening with present day India. Forsaking democratic traditions and mores, the greedy politicians have been harbouring dynastic ambitions and shamelessly nurturing their own families in the political arena.

I did not get even those one hundred bucks from the school on time. Even if I got those, I had no sole lien over those; those were already reserved for this or that demand of my aunt, wily one, if you like to call her.

It so happened in due course that the school management could not afford to pay the wages of the teachers for months together. When I narrated this fact to my aunt, she would not believe. In the meantime, I received a demand from the side of my wife as well, who was parked unauthorisedly at her parental house for almost a year there. I had to send two hundred rupees for her. Not finding any way out to solve this puzzle of life and financial world, I expressed my dilemma to one of my fellow teachers who, in turn, suggested to me that I being the class teacher of a particular class, did collect fees from the class on the fees collection day and that I should, instead of depositing the fees in the school coffers, keep into my pocket the money thus collected. A damn

fool as I ever was, I followed his unscrupulous advice and that particular month I pocketed the entire money collected as fees from the students.

When later somebody asked me as to what about depositing the fees collected to school accounts, I simply refused to fall in line. The school's Head Master, or Principal, as he was known in those days, came to my rescue and support, even as, he was distantly related to my village: he in fact had his wife from our village. His wife was my sister in a sense from village relations. He paid me Rs.200/- and deposited the sum in school a/cs thus squaring my misdeeds off, hushing the embezzlement of school's funds."

"However, you could never pay off that petty sum of two hundred rupees for decades thereafter and the Principal and his wife desperately followed up with you for recovery of their legitimate due, and also, abused you in the worst possible lexicon and expletives throughout the village. But you were shameless enough not to repay their two hundred rupees....", my son added in a peevish tone.

"I did that deliberately. I did not want to repay."

"Why didn't you want to repay? She and her husband were calling you all sorts of names and decried you in the entire village in the foulest terms possible....! Were you not at all ashamed? Whereas I was ashamed despite being a child!"

I kept quiet. My son however continued after a pause: "But that was not a one off instance; you had dozens of such instances wherein the creditors pursued you for recovery of their dues day in and day out. To me, it seemed like a bull chasing the cow for fucking. You took that situation as quite a normal situation. For a shameless person there is no shame: *nang badaa Parmeshwar se* (Fear the devil more than the God)*!* That says volumes about your character and your true colours, as against the normal sanctimonious perception about you in society that you had been all along able to create." He concluded and we engrossed ourselves in the weeding job again.

XXX

4. Shanti Niketan *Of* Naglaa Kath *School*

Enter Protagonist

Having returned from my paternal village, I felt thrilled at the prospect of our having to stay at our maternal village which was a heaven from our perspective indeed. In the hindsight now I feel that my maternal grandfather and his whole family and its members were very kind, civilised and considerate beings. They took every care not to let us feel hurt by their behaviour towards us – mother and son and a sister in the lap of my mother.

The only plausible course of action appertaining to our existence and upkeep was to get me admitted to a school – a primary school – and making my mother virtually a household help for the extended family. My younger maternal uncle – *Chhotey Maamaajee* – being employed at a nearby – not so distant – a city, or one might as well call it a town, his family opted for shifting to that town and stay with him, thereby making room for our stay at *Naanaajee's* home; albeit the house of my maternal grandfather was quite large, by the standards of rural area. This new arrangement might have been a source of constant mental discomfiture for my *Naanaa* and *Naanee,* and also, for other family members, but it was all the more weird for the social set-up.

Why should a married woman, that too, married in a so-called *khaandaanee* (high breed) family, to a sham well-educated youth, stay back at her parents' house? For so long? Unusually long? If there hadn't been any cause of marital rift between the married couple! This was the curiosity that happened to be raised continually throughout that whole year from multifarious corners of society and the village and the area; and it demanded a satisfactory explanation to be proffered every time, with no salutary effect on the countenance of the listeners. My mother used to feel this heat and embarrassment all along, and I, despite being a school going child, too, felt this discomfiture at times. However, I sensed the absurdity of this question and curiosity on the part of society and its curious members; I harboured the notion that because it was the house of my mother's parents, she had every right to live here as long as she willed. Moreover, for the ambience and vibrations of the house in our paternal village were not conducive and congenial, it was all the more desirable that we lived in our maternal village.

By that age, I had not come across the phenomenon of necessaries of life and living, viz; the phenomena of money and property, the phenomena of relationships and their fragility and sham nature *et al.* I had not yet known the phenomenon of sex, seduction and celibacy or the absence of it at all; I had not yet known that it was quite unusual for a youthful lass or lady, particularly, a married one, to remain in forced celibacy yearlong and stay at one's parent's home. Every married woman takes it as a normal routine to have sex quite frequently during the week days, if only not daily. To restrain that tendency due to

compulsions of circumstances is not all that easy and is akin to controlling one's call of Nature, that is, excreta and urine.

Behind the curiosity of people in fact this was the matter of fact. The world does not run in accord with the fancies or idiosyncrasies of school going children!

I was admitted to school which was at the periphery of a nearby hamlet called *Naglaa Kath*. The school was nothing but a brickwork of walls comprising two rooms merely; and a verandah, of course, but without a roof; of course, the rooms were endowed with roofs whatsoever, however, leaky, seepy, not water-proof and not trustworthy at all, particularly, during rains or rainy season. The verandah was parallel to the length of one bigger room and the other room was along the width of this room and verandah combinedly. Of course, there were quite a number of windows which had no grills and doors fitted therein and might pretty well be called rectangular holes or niches in the walls, or might be called wind mills.

In front of this sort of make-shift brickwork of a primary school there was some amount of open space in which there were growing some thickets, nettles and an adult *Peepul* tree which was the main attraction of our school and the only refuge for us all during the summer heat. The open space in school precincts acted as the study ground for us *a la Shaanti Niketan* during the winter season when our solo teacher – *Panditjee–* took us outdoors, outside the ramshackle rooms, to sit in the sunshine and avoid the chill inside.

The teachers in those days were quite benevolent and considerate in that respect, I now feel.

The school was ranged beside the railway track – the *Delhi-Hawrah* railway track -- which was less of a nuisance but more of a source of recurrent entertainment for us curious kids. The not so infrequently plying trains of variegated shapes, sizes, countenances and colours presented an unimaginable as well as other worldly spectacle day in and day out for the eyes of innocent children.

Incidentally for me, the village of my maternal grandparents was also beside the railway track only. Thus it all was sort of a double bonus for me. The frequently plying trains with their rhythmic noise on the rails seemed to be infusing a sense of vigour and dynamism in the milieu of the rural area which was otherwise a somnolent place, had there been no railway tracks or trains. Although at times the trains did play havoc, too, with the physical shapes of the bodies and anatomy of the populace whenever the latter happened to be careless or inadvertent appertaining to the proximity of this technical and engineering automotive wizard – nothing short of a metallic moving monster. It was ruthless as well as merciless!

All around our school, on all the four sides, there were lush green agricultural fields, the reason being that the village in which our school was perched was located on both the sides of the railway track; and between the two portions of the village there was a vast gap on both sides of the track, almost half a kilometre wide. Moreover, the population, too, of the villages was not much, unlike these days. So, our school was situated at a desolate spot, maintaining serenity and privacy of all sorts. The only sound heard there was either that of students and the solo teacher or of the trains hurtling by. The number of trains was also not that high, to be true. Those were rare and their timings were well known to all. By knowing the time in the watch, the people – particularly, our *Panditjee –* could tell which train was to arrive at a particular time. Those were such mesmerising times! Times of punctuality and promptitude!

And not to omit the mention, the arrival of particular trains heralded the onset of our lunch-break, *Rotee kee Chhuttee,* or of the time to call it a day for the schooling. *Panditjee,* however, had no watch – he could not afford one, nor could any of the kids and their parents in the rural milieu. The position of the solar star was the only means to decide the time of the day! And the time for variegated daily chores!

Not to invest any more time to the description of the school – my *alma mater* – let me come to the tale whereby on the first day I was not taken to school by any elder or admitted in any formal manner; rather, I was sent with one of the boys of my age from the maternal village. With the good counsel to the latter that he would tell the *Panditjee* that I would go to school daily and would study there throughout the year, that is, in class five.

With the thrill of going to a more pleasant surroundings of the new school I accompanied my usher, and at school my welcome was encouraging as well, by the seemingly benevolent and kind *Panditjee.*

Now, just see, I am overjoyed with the thought and prospect that I should now stay in my maternal village where there were all the conditions conducive to a wealthy living, lovely surroundings and affectionate treatment, entirely unlike that prevalent at our paternal home – no home, of course, any more, the non-home, in the backdrop of the collapse of our *kutcha* roof and room whatsoever. Here, at maternal village, there was ever present the vast ocean of the affectionate and magnanimous heart of my *Naanee;* there was existent the unfathomable expanse of the firmament of the shelter under my *Naanaa*'s caresses; there was ever extant the kindred and filial love of a maternal uncle for latter's son of one's sister and love and protection for one's sister.

This was the first day of my going to that school, the new school, and in a higher class, that is, class Five. There was a hitch and catch though: the School Leaving Certificate from my previous school had not been procured yet, which was required to fulfil the formalities of the admission. Yet the clout of my maternal family was so high that this lacuna was ignored and I was admitted to school without any fuss further, with only the counsel that the same should be procured and submitted at the earliest. I was, of course, having the mark-sheet of class four obtained from the previous school, that we had collected from the house – or collapsed house – from our paternal village when we had visited there recently. My mark-sheet stood me in good stead since I had secured highest marks, even as, I had stood first in my class four in my last school. I had secured first position in class four; this was a momentous incident for the school, for I had toppled the long-established position and stature of the topper of the class – *Chiranjee* – behind. This phenomenon was all the more noteworthy, for *Chiranjee* was considered to be invincible by that time. Fortunately for *Chiranjee* – and me as well – I had been obliged to leave the school and my village under the weight of Providence and *Chiranjee* most likely might have again continued with his stint as the scholar invincible for his school at that town. With the superior scholar having been removed from the scene by the force of Providence!

If the sun of glory for *Chiranjee* had been released from the eclipse of my presence and intelligence, the one of *Vinod* – my usher at the new school here at *Naglaa Kath* – had set with my emergence there. *Vinod* was the unchallenged champion of his school so far until I shone on the scene. I know, *Vinod* might have felt ill-will and malice towards me as a natural conditioning of human minds. For I had experienced that; when at my previous school I had surpassed the performance of *Chiranjee* during the Half Yearly exam there, scoring highest marks, even higher than *Chiranjee*, there ensued a huge hue and cry, and the family members of *Chiranjee* had created a scene complaining against the school set-up: that I being the

son of a teacher in the town, I had been favoured by the teachers due to teaching class fraternity, that their ward had been given lesser marks deliberately to pull *Chiranjee* down from the topmost position, *et al.*

All bull shit! For the teachers were not aware of my identity by that time, I being a mediocre, rather, a buffoon sort of child by that time. The spectacular turn around was a mystery for me as well; and it was after I had faced the ignominy of that failure, i.e. to solve the 'one plus one' problem, and its aftermath; and the awakening of my inner strengths miraculously under the impact of humiliation by my insolent and insensitive father. Now I feel, it's not always bad that fathers are cruel and insensitive sometimes. It may turn out to be a blessing in disguise, of course, unbeknown to the wards, or unintentionally of the parents.

Not only the parents and family members of *Chiranjee* – who were quite a prosperous family by the standards of that town – but also, us children including myself, whispered amongst ourselves that if what the family members of *Chiranjee* were alleging was true as well as factual, that was very bad; that the teachers ought not to have done so. Bizarre reaction on our part! Standing by the truth! A natural child-like virtue! Even to our own detriment!

5. Nanihaal & Nature's Bounty

Enter Protagonist

It so happened that after his home – whatever it signified – had collapsed in the rains, my father parcelled off his household – his wife and the kids – to the house of his in-laws as he always did, of course, lock, stock and barrel. What treatment, welcome or contempt, did my mother get in its wake in her parent's house, is not a matter worth discussing here; that's obvious enough to a sensible mind. Nevertheless, as for myself, I was so glad to find myself face to face with this eventuality, that was now a reality. In a sense I had as though thanked my collapsed house for the latter's demise! For it was only in the wake of its demise that I had got the Elysian opportunity to live in the heaven of my fancies, that is, the house of my maternal grandparents which was nothing short of the heaven as regards splendour and the sense of well-being, i.e. wealth.

Such a sprawling house of *Naanaajee!* Expansive spheres of habitation, both for humans and for domestic cattle! Creepers of vegetables and small-sized fields growing vegetables and herbs! For sprinting around alike hares, there were very spacious and tidily kept courtyards, foreyards as well as backyards! Residences and agricultural fields! Countless densely shaded trees! It was a tiny hamlet in fact. To call it a hamlet would also be improper. Only a modicum of people of the broader family of *Naanaajee* had come to settle there, with all their pomp and splendour, amidst their agricultural holdings. It presented, in effect, all around a spacious and vast theatrical stage for nature's plays to unfold there, as though! The air there was pristinely pure and unadulterated. They termed it *'Madaiyaa'* (hutment) in colloquial tongue. Everything there resembled an Elysium! Fancy in your childish mind a dreamland and you would find yourself in the midst of my *Naanaajee's* habitations! Or else, just imagine a kingly palace, or the house of *Nand Baabaa* of mythological repute – I mean, just imagine in the manner the rustic folks do if only with a tinge of aristocracy and state of riches, where people do not play servile to the goddess of wealth – *Lakshmee* – where people are not merely the bonded labourers of *Lakshmee,* rather, the *Lakshmee* herself be in attendance at the service of men!

The population of humans was very thin! In such a vast catchment area there were only a few of the inhabitants! It seemed as though only a very thin thread of sound were connecting them all with one another! Looking dwarfish in the sphere of eyesight, the siblings and kith and kin did look like standing at the other end of the string of sound. Yet, bound together in how intimate and natural a connection and affection! Bound by natural and pure love with one another! There every human, or even every creature of any species, did get the same amount of recognition and regard. The habitations where my *Naanaa* dwelt did look like a unique world of mutual trust amongst all the creatures of the Creation!

Then on top of all that, *Naanaajee* himself! And apart from him, there was the towering persona of his elder cousin! Then the impressive and regal personality of his younger cousin! All looked regal in personality! All splendid persona! All had highly pitched baritones – resembling the resounding clouds! When they put on their lengthy *Mirzai* they looked like any great person of the whole world – even more impressive than *Rabindra Nath Tagore* or *Ghaalib!*

The dense overgrowth, thickets and wild vegetation on the rear of the habitations did remind one of the wilderness, a jungle. My child's mind did suggest, 'Certainly it's here only that primordial entities *Aadam* and *Hauwaa* or *Eve – Manu* and *Idaa* – would have sauntered around! This is the very place! Amidst these very thickets and overgrowth! And amidst these only,

we kids had cleared out our little fields – our spheres of work -- creating small beds and sowing therein the seeds of vegetation to our liking. Without any knowledge or regard for the suitability of season or weather for the specific seeds, vegetation or crop.

Clearing some area, where a handful of *Sheesham* trees were already in existence, those trees had been given a tidy and civilized shape, pruning their savage twigs and unruly branches. Presently, when those trees wavered under the stroke of wind, it felt as though they were showering their affection and love on us children who loved them unselfishly so much. Us children, as if they were trying to kiss us and caress us; getting utterly merry, as though feeling very grateful! Of these tall and robust trees, when we levelled the rugged and uneven soil beneath one of these trees, and to render it all the more likeable, when we created a circular platform around it with the help of mud and soil, my mother smeared it with the liquid of cow-dung. It seemed as though the mother earth did lay there embracing her son, the tree! On the occasion and in the season of *Deepaavalee* when it was all salubrious and pleasant all around weather-wise, the platform looked extremely attractive; as though heralding the greatness of our exertions in having given it that likeable shape! My *Naanaajee* did look like a divine personality while standing on that platform, if at all and if only, rarely!

It happened at times that we, the children, did pluck the raw fruits of banana losing our patience with the speed of workings of Nature, and put them inside the burning embers of cow-dung hoping that they would be ripened this way quickly and out of turn – all within this wilderness of thickets, unbeknown to family elders, of course. The result was disappointing, no doubt. Mother Nature does not condescend to oblige by fulfilling childish fancies! Her laws are inviolable, immutable as well as fixed, irrespective of the intents of the doer!

I was admitted to the only school of the nearby hamlet – in grade five, of course.

Now, just see, I am very glad, my morale is very high thinking that I have got to stay at my *Naanee's* village throughout the year, where there is my *Naanee*, the epitome of love and affection towards me, where there is the space of *Naanaajee*'s benevolent shelter, where there is the affection of *Maamaajee* towards his youngest sister, besides the loyalty towards the well-being of the son of the sister! Even calamity was being perceived by me as a good luck!

XXX

6. *Devoid Of Shelter*

Enter Protagonist

This is the first day of my going to school. However, the School Leaving Certificate from my town school has not yet been obtained for completing the chore of admission here. Nevertheless, the marks secured in the grade four – in which I was there during the year gone by – have been obtained; I having secured first rank in the class.

The teachers of my school used to come towards me without any reference and beckoned me telling their colleagues that it was me, that is, the new prodigy of the school. 'There he is! There he is!' I was astonished and felt abashed, also, felt somewhat scared to think why I was being watched and scrutinised like a captive animal or beast of the zoo. To this, my playmates did expound, 'You have secured highest marks; you are the most brilliant student of the class now; you are the sharpest guy now!' I however dreaded that status, 'Oh! But I have done naught; whatever I knew I did only that! Then how am I at fault?' The friends ventured to explain pitying my foolishness, '*Eh, that's a good thing! A welcome development! The teachers are very pleased with you and your performance; they are all praise for you; they are congratulating you, saying wow to you!'

'Is that so! Well!', exclaiming thus I did try to console myself somehow, not sure that what my chums were uttering was not all nonsense.

Nonetheless, not waiting for my annual exam results, I had fled to my *Nanihaal* along with my mother as soon as the summer vacations did start. And there at our paternal village, with the first showers of the rains, my nest, our habitat came crashing down, whatever it was! With that the possibility of returning to our nest at paternal side was blocked totally. So pathetic was the financial condition of my parents, my paternal side! So wretched was the condition of my father! So poor and resourceless he was!

Was he really that wretched financially, sometimes I muse. No! That family was famous for their resourcefulness and influence including wealth: influence never comes *sans* wealth. That was the household of the feudal lords, the warlords of the area, the household wielding their primacy over the plebeians, they being *zameendaars*, the landlords. They were *Mukhiyaas* of the village. They were endowed with big residences, buildings, compounds, male and female residences, all separated, all sprawling all around. And besmirched with all sorts of vices that such families were supposed to be traditionally with!

Nevertheless, ours did have collapsed: the room, shared room, the home for us wretched creatures of that prestigious pedigree! I therefore felt as if all without exception were wretched and poor only, particularly, the family of my own grandfather. For every ancestor is supposed to leave behind some ancestral property, ancestral home for one's coming generations; everybody arranges something on those lines. Also, one must do like that, but my grandfather did not do anything on those lines. He did not care for financial well-being of the family. His wife had died under the stress of financial constraints, I suspect, for my grandfather did not take responsibility for financial and social obligations of his household. Leave apart the property, the house he left as our abode was on the brink of collapse, and it did implode in the first showers of rains during my senses: during the first rains of my coming to senses!

Is it alright for the ancestors to beget issues, to invite issues onto this planet without making arrangement for the latter's habitation, food and clothing? Is that not a foolhardiness and downright unbecoming of them?

Never: this should never be done; lest the progeny instead of saying *'Pitri Devo Bhav!'* (Divine were our ancestors!) should proclaim that 'Our ancestors were

Shaitaans!' (Pitri shaitaano bhav!) As I do!

XXX

7. First Day's Somersault

Enter Protagonist

For my miseries – psychic as well as mental – I blame myself linking these, *a'propos* of the cause and effect phenomenon, to the episode of *Raamveer*, brought up as I have been in a superstitious environment where they believed that every occurrence has a cause behind it.

For no fault of mine I am ever being tortured. Apparently, I see no fault of mine in all this for which I am being penalised and humiliated. I am getting punishment for my having come into existence, as though; I have been paying the price of my existence as though! Yet, this is none of my fault, none of my crime; I am myself a prey, rather; the hunters, the culprits are others, quite other than me: my begetters, my parents, combinedly. For none of them has any sanctity as regards parenthood of mine; that's infructuous. Both of them jointly are accountable to me: for having brought me down on this planet without having first arranged for the basic prerequisites of life, the *Rotee, Kapdaa* and *Makaan*; for having begotten me. Without first creating a solid base, reliable recourse for sustaining the existence on the earth.

Yet our own actions – irrespective of whether those were done deliberately or unknowingly, due to ignorance or negligence – do beg commensurate recompense in the manner of calamities in life; this natural law I have since realised perfectly, even in this very short span of my current life. What is right or what is wrong to do; there is no fool-proof measure to ascertain this in this world, that leads to our actions which may eventually turn out to be crimes or acts punishable by nature, too! In fact, my life-span itself, how long is it yet! Hardly ten years! Of which, the years of activity done of my own volition have been hardly four or five in all. Every incident related to my life I still can recall like the lines on the back of my palms. Of those actions, what was right and what was wrong, or of criminal import, does depend merely on the *sanskaars* that have been inscribed on my psyche by the parents and the society around me. It's quite possible that with the change of the group or society in which I do live, my life eventually might undergo drastic change as regards the concepts of the right and wrong, or of the crime and punishment. Yet, so far as the nature's laws are concerned, I can vouch that none of my actions was worthy of being classified under wrong or unbecoming actions; all were good deeds, worthwhile deeds.

All executed under the inspiration and instigation of the dynamics inherent in the existence itself!

Well, now lo, what significant harm I had done to *Raamveer*, you see – at least I had not done this deliberately, or by design or malice towards him, at all. Nonetheless, his reaction to my mirthful act! His curse bestowed upon me in the wake of that; I was stunned to hear all that coming as it did from his lips; I got perturbed inexplicably, and also, I repented. For my mirthful child-like play. How was I to blame, anyway? How could I guess in advance that this mirthful as well as playful action of mine with *Raamveer* would hurt his sentiments to that extent! I had simply lifted him above the ground, and dropped on the ground spurred by my bodily prowess, strength and effervescent energy. On the dividing line of two agricultural fields, that is, the pavement we were treading on.

XXX

8. *Unintentional Bullyism & Ingrained Casteism*

Enter Protagonist

Nevertheless, it takes time in a new set up for a student to establish one's impression and prestige. In the process, the previously established and gifted students have got to be dethroned or dislodged from their positions, resulting in generation of unhygienic as well as detestable smoke of rancour and envy which is nothing short of any calamity of a great war, reason being that the warriors here in fact are very sensitive as well as susceptible to hurts: tiny trots all, all small-sized kids, girls and boys!

However, the impression of mental strength and aura does get established of its own; it did, within no time. Even if I were to hide the same! The glory is alike the sunshine that can't be hidden, nor can it be helped! It's alike the fragrance of a flower that can't be suppressed! Moreover, on the first day itself the only teacher of that school of *Naglaa Kath* catapulted me onto the seventh sky by way of eulogizing, e.g. uttering, "Oh, wow! This prodigy of a boy, who is very brilliant, has eventually come to our school providentially, as if to boost up the prestige of our school! Now we are sure, we shall be topping all the schools in the area in the exams!"

However happy and gay I might be, why others ought to be happy on this score! That too for a stranger, an unknown student, who was poised precariously to empty their fruit baskets of applause!

Well! The rancour and envy inherent in the minds of students set off showing their fangs. From the nearest blood relations of mine only a boy had been dislodged from his position – *Vinod*. Following the wile counsel of English dictum, i.e. 'to nip in the bud', as though, in the very beginning itself of the session, *Vinod* played a trick upon me to show me down. It so happened that his friend *Raamveer* – I am not sure whether it was his own mischief or the fallout of the instigation by *Vinod* that he did it – tried to crush my foot putting his foot on mine one. Suddenness of the mischief caught me unawares and I sort of squeaked. The accompanying chaps burst into laughter as if to poke me, and I felt piqued. This all happened in class room where our teacher was present. Hearing my squeak, the solo teacher, who was so far eulogizing me so much as though for self-aggrandizement, chose to rebuke me and commanded me to be silent. He did not so much as enquire as to what the matter was, what the causative factor would have been behind that weird behaviour on the part of a gifted chap who had entered the school anew.

Well, as soon as we were let off from the school after closing hours, and as we reached the pavement amidst flora and fauna of the villages, I set off crushing the foot of *Vinod*. Once, twice, time and again, again and again! To support him his friend, *Raamveer*, came forward; he looked quite taller than I was, and I felt somewhat scared for a moment to think of the oncoming prospect. Having no other option left

but to protect myself, I threw my bag away and picked *Raamveer* up on my two arms and dropped him on the ground with the sound of a loud thud.

I myself felt stunned at this turn of events: how did it happen? He fell like a broken dry tree! It did not need application of that much force to subdue him, I now realised. He would have been tamed even by verbal threats.

Following this, both the friends took to their feet towards not the hamlet, their homes, but towards the school itself, shrieking aloud as though some big calamity had struck them, 'Save! Save!!' I however no more harboured any intention to torment them, rather, I was in a mood to beg their pardon for my misadventure and application of excessive force. I felt, *Raamveer* would have been hurt certainly; he had sighed painfully, associating it with a trifling obscene abuse and curse hurled towards me; also, silent curses! But overtly, he did only utter, "Die; you will die! Today itself!" I could however not even laugh or smile contemplating the hurt he might have sustained by virtue of my macho action.

But when both of them were rushing apace – towards the school – then I thought that I too, instead of going homeward, must return to school only – if not anything else, at least to put my point before the teacher. Nonetheless, by the time I reached staggering towards the school, the entire melee of whatever thin population of school was available had assembled at the turn of the corner, the pavement. With the solo teacher standing in their midst! All the pupil ensembled all around! As though not a new student but a beast was looming forth on the pavement towards them! And as though on this prospect all the small kids of the school had taken shelter under the shade of the solo *Gurujee! Aachaaryam Sharanam Gachchhaaami! (a la Buddham Sharanam Gachchhaami!)*

The villainous friend of *Vinod – Ramesh,* who looked burlesque like *Bheem* of *Mahaabhaarat* fame – did come forward to teach me a lesson, uttering, "*Maassaab*! I would see him! I would teach him a lesson! Within no time he would lick the dust on the pavement! All his bullyism would go!" Later on, I was given to understand that his mother – *Ramesh*'s mother – had eloped with someone, her lover, to *Delhi;* nay, elopement implies running away stealthily, i.e. with a sense of guilt in one's heart, in the dark, at night; but she had run away openly, nonchalantly, as though daring the entire community of the tiny habitat.

However, the teacher forbade him rebuking, "No!" I derived a modicum of assurance at this gesture of his – my brand new

teacher.

"*Aachaaryajee!.......*", before I could utter something in defence of my unintentional criminal action, the teacher's sturdy hands had set off punishing by way of resounding slaps my tender, rosy, lovely and child-like cheeks which my lovely and beloved mother kissed and caressed so affectionately almost daily….. *chattt... chattt... chattt...!* Remorseless slaps in the face of an innocent child of hardly ten years of age! Following which, the natural remedy to alleviate the pain did start off in the manner of my crying and sobbing with salty water getting oozed out of my lovely eyes. The slapping pursuit was followed by invariable action of rebukes – the mental punishment -- as if to justify the previous action of physical punishment. He censured my action vehemently as though he was in the wrong in having praised me during the day! As if he could not recognise my true colours during the day; the colours of bullyism! The DNA and genes devilish! The limit of physical punishment had ended at the shedding of my tears; nonetheless, there could be no limit for verbal censures, sky was the limit for that!

The teacher humiliated me and condemned my innocuous action excessively and outrageously, and in those words which were totally unbecoming of him and undeserving of me, 'Consider yourself a bully? Feel yourself very arrogant? Of your body? For we praised you undeservingly that you are very brilliant, very bright! You are not that gifted, I tell you! Here we have so many brilliant students: one more intelligent than the other! Here, your camel would come under the mountain! *(Oont pahaad ke neeche aayega!)* Here you would face the real challenge, real competition! Are you feeling too strong in your physical body which you can't help? For you are from the caste of *Thaakurs?* For you are arrogant about your riches and wealth? Maybe you feel strong, proud and arrogant because you are having too much food and, that too, gratuitously at your *Naanaa*'s! You beat our polite and gentle kids! On first day itself so much mischief; what will happen in the coming days? We can't teach you in our school; go tell *Thaakur Saahab! Eh, Vinod! Eh Raamveer!* Do tell *Thaakur Sahab* on my behalf that we cannot afford to keep and teach this *Shaitaan*, this brat of a boy at our school! He does torment our students... he may kill them even..... who knows!'

Entirely and starkly nonsense! Entirely baseless unreasonable allegations and accusations! Against a small innocent child, who had unintentionally done something unusual, the cause of which he himself was unable to fathom!

Entirely one-sided judgement! Without listening to both the sides of the tale! This was tantamount to murder of justice in entirety! *ab initio!* This was tantamount to the sinful and unpardonable tendency on the part of adults to crush the morale of an innocent child! This sort of tendency does find place with a *Shaitaan* only. My child's brain was totally unable to fathom the import of the terms like 'ours', 'gentle', 'innocent', '*Shaitaan*' etc. used recklessly by my teacher, on the very first day of my new school. I reasoned in my mind that I was a student of his school now, how could he call me a stranger, an outsider, then? Am I still an outsider? Am I still a product of casteism: a *Thaakur;* (our teacher was a *Braahman*)? How could he call those children gentle whereas they had jealously tried to humiliate and hurt me by crushing my foot in the class during the day? How could I be called a *Shaitaan* whereas in my heart, too, there was surging forth a pathos for the aggrieved children, my purported enemies? Of course, after facing such barrage of harangue against me from the side of my teacher that tender feeling had subsided to a considerable extent.

Nevertheless, in the wake of this episode I developed in my mind a notion – a weird one at that – forever that I was a child with ample amount of bodily strength, that I could fling even sturdy lads like *Raamveer* down, that the latter would ever be in the scare of me, that my path for future had been rendered fearless and easy, and that my future was secured now. And everybody knows that there is no notion as pleasurable and as assuring as that of freedom and fearlessness! If one is strong, if one is blessed with the strength and prowess – of all sorts – the worldly safety and security would be at one's disposal; also, the worldly peace and tranquillity would lick one's feet. The ubiquitous tendency of exploiting, torturing, tormenting, even killing others, and eating others as one's staple food that is there prevalent in the entire world of living creatures, would no more affect a person endowed with *Shakti* (strength, prowess and resourcefulness). No one would gather courage to tease or trouble one. And what else is joy or pleasure in life? Isn't that this one only?

XXX

9. *Barn & Summer Heat*

Enter Naanaajee

My youngest daughter having been deported back to my house from her husband's crumbled nest, and his only ten year old son having sought admission in the school in the nearby hamlet beside the railway track, it was a sultry day of summer when I was scheduled to thresh the barley crop in the barn.

The harvest – whether it be wheat or be it the barley, wheat, of course, was very scarce, it was predominantly coarse grains and millets etc. which were grown by the plebeians those days, wheat came in prominence one year later in 1968 - it was 1967 that we were in – were supposed to be threshed under the hooves of domestic bullocks. My eldest son and I were never comfortable working together and as a result were seldom on talking terms, the latter being a temperamental youth, easily irascible and always poised for rebuking the kids and the womenfolk of the household. He was definitely lacking something as regards grey matter in his skull. Illiterate he indeed was; merely able to decipher the words of *Geetaa* that he kept in his *kutcha* room which he resided in.

It was late afternoon – around 4:00 p.m. or so – and the time to go work in the fields or accomplish other daily chores related to rustic as well as agrarian living. It need not be reiterated that all around there used to be the feeling of well-being and happiness, feel good, so to say, with sprawling habitations and large land-holdings under the ownership of every one of us blood relations. Seeing that my eldest son had not yet gone to the barn with the bullocks, I took lead – I was quite active by that time and was actively engaged in household activities – and took the bullocks to the barn. Those were the days of relative honesty; the incidents of petty thefts were rare, especially, in our area, given our influence. All the necessary implements required for the threshing of harvest in the barn were kept lying there in the barn itself, without any risk of their being made off with by the neighbours or strangers. I reached the barn, yoked the bullocks and set off driving them around the circular-shaped heap of the unthreshed harvest.

Quick came my grandson, that is, the son of my youngest daughter, hardly ten years of age, rushing towards the barn. Wrapping a scarf around his small skull, to ward off the burning sunshine and sultry summer heat. He was very much enthused to partake of the agricultural activity with me. Actually, in his village, there used to be no such opportunity to indulge in agricultural chores, for his father abhorred physical labour. Also, his father did not permit womenfolk and children to venture out of the four walls of the claustrophobic habitat. Therefore, this young lad, when he saw the opportunity come his way for the first time, even as, he had come to realise that he would be staying here only for the coming year, he felt glad and might have decided to contribute to the physical labour alongside us.

He proclaimed to me, "*Baabaa*, I shall help you in driving the bullocks for threshing the harvest."

"Oh, that's really awesome! Great!.... By the way, who sent you here?..." I probed further without any purpose, and merely as a matter of bantering.

"My mother sent me saying that you were alone here, so I must come and help you in this task."

I gave him simpler tasks in keeping with his tiny capacities, like, moving around the circle accompanying the bullocks; throwing up the strewn hey with the help of the forks onto the heap under the feet of the bullocks etc. And he was deriving extreme pleasure in these activities, oblivious of the scorching heat of the sun and the perspiration that had wetted his scarf and the clothes. Possibly, in the childhood, the sense of heat and cold is felt lesser or is not felt at all.

When we were indulged in the task like this – the grandpa and the grandson – an acquaintance of ours from the nearby village happened to pass thereby, also, a relative of ours – the brother-in-law of my sons – happened to pass by, and seeing us busy in the strenuous task, they both stopped to chat with us. Also, they expressed appreciation on seeing this young chap enthusiastically engaged in threshing work in the barn with me.

In fact, they even relieved him of the strenuous task and helped me to some extent in the strenuous task, asking the boy to take rest under the shade of fruit-bearing trees beside. Need not be mentioned that the soil being very fertile, there were shaded trees aplenty all around. There was no dearth of shaded trees and cool shade in the catchment area of the village, including those around our threshing ground, the barn.

I asked my grandson to go play in the village telling him that I myself would take care of the task, but he did not budge. He was deriving unprecedented pleasure from the job, and also, a sense of pride in contributing to the physical tasks which he had never done in his paternal village. People think that physical labour is a menial job and abhorrent task, but the fact is that physical labour is as essential for mental and physical pleasure as rest and relaxation are.

It was when the boy was extremely glad that my elder son was seen coming from the side of the village with his usual scarf wrapped around his sturdy peasant's skull and with his robust and rough arms swinging along. The boy was still expectant that his enthusiasm would be appreciated and that he would still be permitted to show his feats at the barn; however, that was not to be. My rough and tough son commanded him to leave the task and go play in the village. The boy hesitated for a while, but given the tough countenance of my elder son, he had no other option but to run towards the hamlet and busy himself with his child playmates under the shade of groves of trees.

XXX

10. Elder Maamaa, *A Terror*

Enter Protagonist

Whereas it was a treat to be in my maternal grandparents' village, and there was no possibility of ever suffering the pangs of hunger and wretchedness, or collapse of house or huts, there still were dreads and hazards to this otherwise unblemished pleasure. One such trouble – and incessant and ever present one – was our elder *Maamaajee*. He was a terror incarnate in himself. So much so that even our *Naanaajee* was not at talking terms with him, given his tantrums and quarrelsome nature. He was in the habit of rebuking children for this reason or that, or even without any plausible reason: merely on trivial excuses. I never found him amiable or congenial towards kids and womenfolk, except his mother whom, of course, he could not rebuke. Mother is such an adorable entity. And my *Naanee* indeed was a very affable soul, an ever smiling face!

He used to rebuke his wife quite frequently and sought any

pretence whatever to rebuke and create tantrum at the time of having food in the kitchen. Kitchen actually was not a small-sized kitchen in urbanite sense: it was a big hall in which at least five kitchens of the size of those found in ordinary families could be fitted. He used to rebuke the children if the latter were found merry-making on the way when he would be going towards the home: in the morning for breakfast, or the first meal of the day; and in the evening for dinner, or the second as well as the last meal of the day. There was no concept of breakfast or lunch or dinner in the family traditions; merely first meal and the second meal, none in-between. Well, of course, the young ones had liberty to have three or four meals in a day, and they did too. Including me! Not the elders of the household; and they kept hale and hearty by virtue of this abstemiousness. Our *Maamaajee* was, too. But he was misutilising his good health for doing *akushal karmas*. He behaved like a devil.

He rebuked even my mother not-infrequently: on this or that frivolous pretexts. And I found my mother ever in the dread of that daemon of a man. She never minced her words in proclaiming thus in his absence, 'He is a daemon, a *raakshas*!' Because he was ever seen dressing her down, hurting her self-esteem. Why only her, he used to misbehave even with her own issues

– girls mostly, for he had only one son who was the eldest amongst his siblings, and did not talk to his father, having revolted against the latter's unreasonable behaviour – and also, with the issues of his younger brother, remorselessly.

How could I be spared! I was no exception to his lashes of tongue. Of course, he never used his hands or legs to beat anybody. But the verbal punishment was no less tortuous! He made us children work in the agricultural fields, and for this, he would choose the time when we were busy in our childish games. He sort of derived a sadistic pleasure in disturbing and upsetting the children's psyche.

If ever he saw us children taking bath at the hand-pump in the cattle compound where it was very cool and shaded, and if he observed us using bathing soap on our bodies, he would ask us coldly and in a sarcastic manner, "Does the soap make the face *Malook* (shining and pretty)?" And we innocent children didn't have courage to respond either in yes or no. It was a torture to be in sight of him.

We children at times were obliged to muse that if our elder *Maamaajee* had not been there on the planet, and particularly, in our *Nanihaal*, our lives would have been much peaceful and accomplished. He was like an anathema in the lives of the members of the household, particularly womenfolk and children. His ever unsettling presence reminded me of the equally unwanted presence of our father on paternal side, and all our enthusiasm and pleasure of having that bully of a man behind was diminished when we found the equally ferocious a beast here at our *Naanee's*. It seems, God had ordained our fate to be like that only!

It's not that our *Maamaa* was bad for us only; he was equally a nuisance for the inhabitants of the village and the area. Intermittently, he would be buying tussle with this person or that for no issues of any substance or consequence. In fact there was something amiss as regards his grey matter.

Once it so happened that he bought a scuffle with the elder brother of *Ramesh* – the same legendary lad in the school whose mother had run away with her paramour to *Delhi*. The young lad was hauling the piles of sugarcane on his head from a field to the crusher in his village. His field was beside the field of our *Maamaajee,* and for going to village, the path was through the embankment of *Maamaajee's* field. Now, with load on the head if the lad did swagger once in a while onto *Maamaajee's* field, allegedly crushing the crop of *Maamaajee,* it was not tolerable to the irrational *Maamaajee.* It did not enter his youthful and adult mind

that negotiating on the thin line of muddy embankment it was quite natural that the person would do fouls if only unintentionally. Nevertheless, *Maamaajee* used his foul as well as acerbic tongue against the youth. Unmindful that a youth is a youth! The youth pulled out a sugarcane from his bundle and struck twice or thrice on the back of *Maamaajee.* There ensued so much tumult, hue and cry, obviously.

In the aftermath of this incivility on the part of that youth, our *Maamaajee* took many initiatives as if to salvage the lost prestige – of having been beaten by an urchin. He contacted his strongmen relatives; strongmen in the sense of bullyism and those who could wield sticks and use firearms nonchalantly against their enemies. One such source of strongmen was the village called *Fatehpur.* As the name suggested, the inhabitants of that village prided in having vanquished some *Muslim* enemies from their village and made them to flee from their village, that's why the name *Fatehpur*, i.e.; the village of victors. Some seniors of that village visited the village of our *Maamaajee* and threatened the father of the erring lad with dire consequences. The lad had already fled from the village for fear of definite reprisals from the side of strongmen that our *Maamaajee's* family definitely were.

Nonetheless, the

disreputable drama of revenge and rancour came to an end when the son of our *Maamaajee* did finally avenge the humiliation of his father. He had taken upon himself the challenging task of taking on the ruffian lad. He was, as a matter of fact, constantly on the lookout for the lad, the culprit, and had always been carrying a knife in his pocket, *a la* that shown in films. One afternoon, unfortunately for the lad, our *Maamaajee's* son did sight him near his fields doing some field chores. He took the son of his uncle – my younger *Maamaa*'s son – along with him and accosted the lad bravely there and started wielding the fists including knife on the culprit. He let him flee only when he had given him ample amount of thrashing. However, a neighbour as well as an acquaintance of the lad came to his rescue, who started taking sides with the lad and the latter did ultimately run away. Ran away not only from the clutches of my maternal cousins, but also, from the area itself, and was never again seen there, at least during my memory and stay there.

Nevertheless, my *Maamaajee* could not mend his ways, and he remained ever an irascible adult and kept on quarrelling and squabbling with one man or the other now and then not infrequently. Why only men, even with women! We, the close relatives, were ever at his hit

list and ever at receiving end, and we disliked him no end, too.

And one would wonder to be enlightened that my *maamaajee* was considered to be a *swaamee*, a virtual sage, an accomplished person of previous births. By character, his appellation was befitting only; he would get up invariably in the wee hours of the early morning, possibly at four, and then would take bath on the open air well-head beside the residence, by fetching water from the dug-well with the instrumentality of a bucket, a pail, with the help of a straw rope. Appreciably as well as amazingly, this schedule of his daily routine never faced any disruption, the changes of weather and season, those of temperature or air, notwithstanding. Whether it be chilled cold of wintry season, or it be the scorching and sultry heat of summer season, *swaameejee* was never seen flinching from his daily routine of taking bath at the well-head in the wee hours of the dawn; at a time when all others around the well would be sleeping in the comforts of their couches and quilts. So far so that even those in the beds felt a chilling sensation in their spine when our *maamaajee* poured bucketfuls of water on his head standing erect semi-naked on the well-head, and accompanying the same with, of course, recitation of some spiritual hymn or prayer, mostly the refrain: *'Tere poojan ko bhagwaan, banaa man mandir aaleeshaan!'* (For the sake of your adoration only, O God Almighty, this consciousness of ours has been created!). Apart from such strictness in routine, he was extremely abstemious in the matters of eating; he had food only twice a day. Perfectly rule-bound in fact!

And such a *swaamee* was what he was, as delineated above!

XXX

11. Naanee *Humiliated By My Father At* Veerpuraa

Enter Naanee *(Maternal Grandmother)*

Almost eight months had elapsed since when my daughter had been staying at our home forsaken by her indolent and worthless husband. For none of her fault, it was all the fault of us, her parents, having wedded her to such a good for nothing family. On top of that, they claimed themselves to be *'Khaandaanees'* (i.e. of fine breed, pedigreed, so to say). Unable to even take care of their families and claiming grandeur! Shame on them! Pure hypocrisy! But by the time the realisation dawned upon us, it was too late already. The entire money given to my daughter by us in the manner of dowry had been grabbed or usurped, if you like, by the father-in-law of my second daughter who was incidentally my youngest daughter's sister-in-law, in relation. The joint family system had all such

pitfalls; anybody could go scot-free after perpetrating such familial misappropriations!

During this one year of my youngest daughter's stay at ours, I sensed that the villagers and people of the area suspected something fishy about the relationship between my daughter and her husband; and it was quite natural. Stay of a married young woman at her parents' home for yearlong was indeed a matter of gossip for those who had no other chores than this one.

This was under such circumstances that I once planned a visit to my parents' village. Incidentally, the school where the husband of my daughter worked as an *ad hoc* teacher was in the same village, that is, my parental village. This village – *Veerpuraa* -- and the village – *Somnaa* -- where her husband stayed with his uncle and aunt were in close proximity only. I had no other specific purpose to visit my brother's house – my parents had long expired – except to see the husband of my daughter and to smell the scent of his intentions. The latter had no wherewithal or skills at all to build a house or even a hut, nor did he seem to have any intention to possess a house of his own, forget about wherewithal.

I visited my brother's house during the festive season of *Deepaawalee* and intended to meet my son-in-law there. First my intention was to call him at my brother's home, but an insolent lad as he was he did not oblige, nor did he show any courtesy or politeness to suggest any other proposition. Left with no other option, I ventured to go to the school where he worked, and in this pursuit my brother accompanied me, too. We reached the school and requested the staff there to call the lad. The staff approached and advised the lad, but he did not so much as show the courtesy to come and speak to us. Instead, when we insisted that we wanted to see him, he came fretting and fuming and called us names before the staff, also denying any link or relationship with us. This was quite humiliating. Beyond our forbearance power! I felt hurt, deeply hurt; and my brother too felt very much annoyed at the incivility of this lad who, incidentally, was the husband of my dear and lovely daughter.

In the heat of his anger and madness, he used language like 'this vulgar old lady has come here, she is not related to me' *et al*; in fact, coming from a feudal system as he did, he considered us village folks as someone of lower strata and lower breed. Whereas indeed he himself was of lower breed and uncivil as exhibited by his misdemeanour! Our humiliation was in the face of school staff, and my brother's family was quite a respectable family too in the village. We felt deeply hurt.

Anyway, there was no solution to this incivility and insolence on the part of a feudal lad, that too, our son-in-law; and we came back fretting and fuming no end.

On returning to my village after a few days, I narrated the whole ugly episode to my sons and family with lot of anguish as I indeed felt. Hearing this episode of humiliation of their mother and maternal uncle at the hands of the husband of their youngest sister, however beloved, they got enraged, and they called all sorts of foul and non-foul names to that lad who incidentally was inexorably linked to us as the husband of my beloved daughter. This incivility of the husband of my daughter became a chattering point, a staple stuff, for gossiping for weeks together for the village folks.

XXX

12. Like Father Like Son: Son Pays For The Sins Of Father

Enter Protagonist

I was studying in school at the nearby village in standard 5th while staying at my maternal uncle's home during that one year – 1967, to be precise. In fact, while staying there in that situation when we were living as parasites, as refugees, as wretched persons, it never crossed my mind that the house I was living in did not belong to us, and that we were living there as a burden on that family. Fortunately for us – me and my mother – the parents of my mother – my maternal grandpa and maternal grandma – were still alive and being the owners of the entire landed estate as yet nobody dared say anything contemptuous to my mother or me and my younger sister. Moreover, by now, the distance between the marriage of my mother, that is, the point of her separation from this house as an equal partner in the ownership of the house, and the year she was obliged to stay back here again compelled by circumstances, was not long, merely fifteen years; and she was quite young and youthful still. She commanded lot of clout in the affairs of the family. Not only influence, even the tyranny, so to say, towards her sisters-in-law, she used to show alongside her mother who was also an adult only by that time and afflicted with the notion of conventional wisdom that daughters-in-law must needs to be kept under tab and tight leash of the mothers-in-law, and the only effectual way to ensure this was tyranny.

In hindsight, now when I ponder over those past years, I feel, that though no one there showed any discrimination or antagonism towards us three – me, my sister and my mother – there would have been an undercurrent of dislike towards us. For we were subject to our elder maternal uncle's ire not infrequently. Not only this, our maternal uncle was not infrequently very harsh and cruel towards his sister too, that is, my mother. And we felt lot of heat and annoyance at such treatment. My mother was quite often heard lamenting, "He is a daemon incarnate!" commenting on the behaviour of her elder brother. For small small and ignorable excuses, too, he chastised her and us as well during that one year of our parasitic living thereat.

One day, when my *Naanee* (maternal grandmother) returned from her maternal village, we were very glad as she was an affectionate lady and possessed an ever smiling countenance. However, this time she was not amused and this demeanour on her part was quite peculiar and abnormal for us. She was narrating the episode of her humiliation at the school of *Veerpuraa* at the hands of some person incidentally called my father, to the family and, particularly, to her sons, both of whom were there present eventually. My younger *Maamaajee* was employed at a nearby town in fact and as usual he had come at the weekend to his village. On hearing of the humiliation by my father of their mother they got enraged, very angry and upset, and said all sorts of bad things and called all sorts of bad names to my father. They recalled all the evil habits, indolence and characteristics of my father, in which, now the insolence had been added as an insult to injury.

Not only this, they beckoned to me too uttering, "Your *Baap* (father) is such a scoundrel and rascal; he does not even know how to behave! Behave with the elders of the family and relatives!" *blah, blah.*

This treatment meted out to me was entirely at divergence with the treatment of unflinching affection I had been showered with thus far. When it comes to individual's own discomfort or dent to one's prestige, I realised, all the relationships do melt away and dissolve within no time. Within a moment's time-gap we were feeling as though we were strangers and wholly unwelcome folks in the same household, in which, we were staying since long without a hint of such malice ever having been shown towards us.

My young mother indeed felt quite embarrassed in such a situation. She merely exclaimed, "I already told you that he is an unworthy and indolent husband! Insolent, too! Very bad man!"

And with this, simultaneously as well as subconsciously, I recalled the scene of my father wielding a thick wooden log on the back of my docile mother insensitively and the wooden stick getting broken in the

tyrannical feat. What a daemon! I thought, but how to get out of his clutches, I wondered.

XXX

13. Guddee: *My Fair Sex Hypersensitivity*
Enter Protagonist

Despite my having been meted out a contemptuous treatment by the solo teacher – the *Panditjee* – of the school, I had made it to the school nonchalantly the next day ignoring the whole hog of slapping, rebukes, threats and the ultimatum as to rusticate me from the school and resultantly not letting me continue in the school. We had reached the school before time the next day; *Vinod* had now become my chum, he might have thought it prudent to be friends with a bully sort of a lad. *Raamveer* did turn coward as regards dealings with me. Nonetheless, all of us reached the school all together.

In fact the drama of previous day's childish fighting had not ended in the school; it had continued to the village, to the home of *Raamveer* in that I accompanied him to his home too. Possibly to offer an explanation for my action. On hearing the entire episode, *Raamveer*'s mother very gently as well as politely counselled me that I being a strong child, it was incumbent upon me to be careful about dealing with other weaker children physically, lest they should get hurt. Also, that I ought to treat his son kindly as a child should treat another child. I felt highly impressed by her kind gesture and vowed never to torment her son. However, her approach was quite at variance with that of our teacher and was therefore much more effective. That was just like an approach of a mother, showing as much tenderness towards the same-aged son of another mother as she showed towards her own son. This interaction left a lasting impact on my psyche. Thereafter, I felt having been relieved of a heavy burden from my heart which had been created by the treatment of the teacher.

My mother however simply laughed the entire childish episode off.

As we reached the school, not too much later thereafter, *Guddee* too arrived. And she was sighted by me slinging her bag on her tender and shapely shoulders and then taking the same down. The process seemed quite engrossing and enchanting. I observed that the countenance of *Vinod* had become excited on seeing her. *Raamveer* somehow as if finding nothing sensible to do started nudging *Vinod* whispering, of course, audibly, 'Lo, she is there! Thy beloved friend has come!' *Vinod,* in turn, rejoindered in a voice affected with love: "Come

on, *Guddee,* do come here! Why keep standing there?"

Guddee did step towards us and stopped beside us. Alike a speck from the room of beauty of God! She was not the student of our class or grade in fact; she was one class behind us. The previous day when I had come she was not seen there, and I could not make any idea about such a beauty being available in the school. On seeing her today, I felt as if it were a double bonus for me: to have such a beautiful lass in the school, on top of the good fortune of having to stay at *Naanaa's* home! I, however, set off musing, 'Well, it was for the good of mine that I got the beatings and floggings yesterday itself; *Guddee* did not see me in that bad light! Being beaten, being called bad names, all my vices being reeled out, lest she would have.....'

"*Guddee!* Let's introduce you to him! He is the son of my *Buaajee,* he will study here only this year," *Vinod* was apprising her whereas I was thinking how attractive and seductive that young lass was! What control could I have on getting attracted towards the beauty of a girl! The lass herself was piercing me with the arrows of her feminine attraction. The fair sex itself was to blame for this, not me, the small child. Boys were not to blame! If there is something amiss in all this, something immoral, something sinful or criminal in this phenomenon, the phenomenon of a boy getting enchanted by the beauty of a young girl, this is the fault of the God; God Himself seems to be amorous minded; He is to blame! O man! You ought to punish God Himself, not the innocent man who is merely a puppet in the hands of God for performing actions! Why do you dub the idols who have been created by God Himself, totally dependent on Him, absolutely helpless, simply the idols suffused with consciousness, as culprit, as immoral, and why do you torment them?

Or, maybe the traditions, convictions and opinions of human race itself are wrong, are false, aren't true, are preposterous! The propensity of human race to tinker with the laws of nature, to ban the natural tendencies by way of legal or conventional injunctions, is unwelcome, unbecoming and abominable, and also, worth forsaking forthwith.

I didn't deliberately intend that I should like *Guddee*, or as they say, love her; yet she was getting loved by me, my heart and mind. Unbeknown to me and unintentionally, even within no time she and her beauty overwhelmed the whole of my existence – submerging whole of my psychic existence under her influence and aura. I started liking her, every action of hers, her countenance, her subtle gestures. I started liking her melodious voice! In totality she stood before me as a *Vasheekaran Mantra* – a *mantra* that facilitates seduction of an opposite sex! I, in turn, was obliged to stare at her only as a hapless and helpless lad of ten!

Now, you only decide how I am to blame in all this rigmarole, in all this love affair? If at all I am to blame, it is the fault of this carnal body of mine that, in turn, has been created by God, or which has been begotten by my worldly parents; they only are the *Brahmaa* of my carnal body inside which I find myself dwelling! I too shall attain the stature of a *Brahmaa* one day or the other by merging with some better half! I am the better half or a part of *Brahmaa*, too!

I have little command over the actions being done by this carnal body and its organs. I cannot modify its actions or proclivities at all. I am merely a wayfarer of this carnal body: a '*Videh!*'

Well, if the natural and innate tendency on the part of human beings to get affected by or to get enamoured of the beauty and charm of the fair sex as well as a seductive lady is a sin or crime in the eyes of man, every wayfarer of carnal body is a sinner or criminal. I do not intend to produce any proof for this accusation of mine; this can be felt by every wayfarer of body within one's own body itself.

"Well! What's your name?" Wow! If there were any categories of the voice, this was the voice of top category – emerging from the source of sound with *Guddee*, flowing from the lotus petals of her tender and pink hued lips, arriving unto the ears of mine, drenching them with the shower and rain of nectar!

That she wanted to know my name, this feeling itself was so enthralling and elevating! Then definitely she would have been impressed by my personality and countenance, too!

'Arvind' it was *Vinod* only who apprised her; I however could not utter a word, abashed and blushed as I was feeling in front of the fair sex. I started looking sideways so as to avert her gaze, lest she should notice my countenance blushing. My eyes did rise towards the lofty sky: as if trying to grope in the dark of unfathomable, illimitable, unending and unknowable one!

Thereafter I could never gather courage and guts to converse with *Guddee* throughout the year, as I had never been whenever it came to conversing with the fair sex, why only *Guddee*! Why only the first day! On that day, too, it was *Vinod* only who had continued the channel of conversation with her, even on my behalf. *Vinod,* rather, did converse with her throughout the year and whenever he liked to, without any hitch or hesitation. As for me, whenever I saw her coming, or whenever she came within my sight, I felt a fit of awkwardness overpowering me, a queer thrill running down my spine, as though the vital energy of my life itself were standing before me in physical form as an incarnation! Nevertheless, the causative factor behind this awkward, abnormal and unseemly behaviour of mine was the tape fitted within my subconscious mind by my upbringing whereby it was ingrained in my psyche that 'one should shun the company of and conversation with the girls or fair sex'. I could never gather courage or cudgels even to look towards her, what to speak of talking to this fairy of a lass, damsel of a girl. It seemed as though the blossoms did waft the breeze of fragrance all around, yet the bumble bee did keep on merely staring around!

Nevertheless, in my whole tenure of grade fifth, I had never for even a moment let her portrait be removed away from the gallery of my mind and heart. She became a source of inspiration for me, a source of creativity and positivity; in her presence, I became extremely self-conscious. I did feel enthused whenever I sighted her around: near or far. When I did secure highest marks in the exam I felt a thrill to think that *Guddee* would feel impressed by my feats; that an attraction would be engendered in the heart of *Guddee* towards me due to my accomplishments. I wonder whether this phenomenon was accountable for my gradual success in securing more and more marks throughout the year. Nonetheless, I feel, no girl, leave apart an unparalleled damsel, would like to love a lad who were dependent on others for his education, living, clothing and everything, just like a parasite, merely a creature devoid of shelter, howsoever, gifted one might be. I was after all merely a wretched chap making do with living at my *Naanaajee*'s house!

XXX

14. Cursive Writing

Enter Protagonist

Unlike these days, our teacher – *Panditjee* – those days used to command us daily to do some cursive writing. For, only single language was in vogue by that time in the newly independent country – the mania for English tongue had not taken wings as yet – we children were under the impression that cursive writing was an unavoidable daily chore of schooling methodology. The intent behind resorting to cursive writing and according so much importance to such a monotonous chore as filling at least one page daily was,

frankly speaking, not clear to us children. Now when my handwriting has assumed the proportions of a spider's scrawling path, even as, my hands and head quiver while writing anything on paper, and my brain and temples around my ears get extremely strained in the process, in hindsight, now I feel that the cursive writing was very crucial to my success in later life. Due to the practice of cursive writing my handwriting had become quite attractive and pretty at that time, and retained its glamour for decades together thereafter.

My own handwriting attracted the appreciation of the solo teacher invariably daily.

However, like in other aspects of life, the school scenario and set up also keep on changing with time. In the interregnum of the months, there came another teacher to the school apart from our *Panditjee.* He was a young chap unlike our oldie teacher; and was therefore impartial as well, without showing any proclivity towards me or towards the established notions.

My teacher – *Panditjee* – never pointed out any mistakes in my cursive writing, rather, gave 'Good' remark once in a while, too. And I felt puffed up as if that were true. Now in hindsight, I feel, that was simply a trick of the teacher and that depended on his whims and mood; it had no correlation with the ground reality in fact.

One day when the *Panditjee* had proceeded on leave and the young *Turk* was in command, on being presented the notebook of cursive writings to him, dispassionately as well as impartially, he pointed out certain lacunae in my otherwise impeccable handwriting. That was an anathema! A taboo! How could a teacher point out my errors! I felt revulsion towards the otherwise revered teacher.

When I disclosed the 'sin' and 'impropriety' of the young teacher to my companions – the classmates – they took umbrage too, against the 'improprieties' of this young stranger! Who was not aware of the established conventions as well as notions of the pedigreed schooling! The remaining day passed unhindered somehow, that is uneventfully thereafter.

Nevertheless, I carried the affront of the innocent teacher unto my home. Even if I had not done so, my compatriots were too excited and outraged to check them from keeping the episode with grave implications to themselves; they divulged the 'serious' matter to my maternal siblings and cousins. They felt offended, in turn.

Next day, inevitably, the retributory action was to be taken: the young stranger was to be taught manners! How to behave with the established pedigree of the school! My cousins – *Maamaa*'s daughters -- and a few others accompanied me to the school the next day. Those were the days of winter season and resultantly, the classes were held in the open, under the sun's warmth. Our teacher was squatted at the well-head, enjoying sunshine, unsuspecting of the imminent childish storm – thunderstorm, rather. He could never have dreamt in his wildest dreams that such an innocuous act as pointing out certain errors and suggesting certain corrective measures in the notebook of cursive writing of a child could engender so much tumult as well as dissent in the otherwise tranquil school.

On reaching the school, the retinue surrounded the teacher at the well-head and started reasoning with him, advocating my case. The teacher was befuddled. He tried to reason with this elf-army but to no end. They were hell bent upon making the teacher relent and make amends, that is, saying that everything done by me in my notebook was alright. No questions asked, so to say!

The drama continued for quite a while; and thereafter, the teacher started enjoying the tussle. He started deriving perverse pleasure in this childish activity. For now it was in his powers to end this squabble or to continue with it unendingly. Finally, when it was too much, and he felt that the school must start functioning sanely, he struck off whatever he had written and the retinue fled feeling victorious. A sham sense of bravado and grandeur!

However, this was not a one off episode, where my bloated false ego exhibited itself, there were several other occasions when on my behalf my well-wishers took umbrage to squabble with the teacher on this issue or that. Another such occasion arose when in the examination of art, the drawing, another lesser mortal was awarded more marks on his coloured picture. Obviously, his drawing as well as colouring was far superior to mine one, I felt in heart. But because I was brilliant student in all other subjects, I and my fans, my well-wishers, my votaries, felt that none else had any right to secure more marks than I did in any of the subjects whatsoever. Queer logic! Brilliant in one subject, brilliant in other subject, rather brilliant in all the subjects, too!

However, the reasonable teacher tried his best to reason with my fans that it was true that I was most brilliant in some crucial subjects as arithmetic and language, nonetheless it was not necessary that I should be good at drawing and arts as well. But who could convince the *Vaanar Senaa* (the army of apes and

baboons)! Their seemingly logical reasoning was that, for I was the most brilliant chap of the school, I must be brilliant in arts as well, in all the subjects, rather, and thus liable to be awarded the highest marks, irrespective of whatever quality my performance might be of! Though I derived satisfaction from such illogical mental scuffles with the innocent and impartial teacher on the part of my fans, somewhere in my heart I felt at that time too that the drawing and the piece of art of the other student was really superior to and better than mine one.

XXX

15. Yashodaa & Daamodar

Enter Protagonist

While living in the house of my maternal grandparents I had little idea that the house I was living in was not my 'own house' in worldly sense, in the sense of social conventions. This realisation dawned quite later in life, rather, it dawned when I had reached High School. Wasn't it too late for a sane skull? My father was reportedly teaching as an *ad hoc* teacher in *Veerpura,* and I was least bothered about that aspect as well. My maternal grandparents were alive, and my young lovely mother was there to worry about all such matters concerning me and my heritage. If at all I had any! No one had cudgels either in the household or even outside its precincts to make me realise that the same was not my house, and more so, that I was in fact living in refuge: under the condescending tutelage of my maternal grandparents, quite possibly the latter suffering or having to do with the annoyance as well as grievances of the latter's sons and daughters-in-law in this behalf.

The household of my *Naanaa-Naanee*, it seems, was the richest one in the area – the catchment area – of the small village; and was therefore a respectable lot amongst the inhabitants. They were sort of princes and princesses of the area, figuratively put. Wherever or whenever they treaded or passed through the paths, people showed their extreme reverence and invariably behaved quite reverently towards them. Be it the elder *Naanaajee*, or be it my real *Naanaajee,* or be it their youngest cousin – also, one more *Naanaajee* of mine! All were gifted with impressive personalities by God, or by Nature, to be precise. For gents were revered, it was but natural that their female folks would be revered, too, and they did.

Moreover, a striking feature of the social milieu in my *Nanihaal* was that there was no restriction imposed on the women folks for venturing out of the precincts of the

homesteads; they not only ventured out of the homesteads, but also, were a great support in conducting the household and agriculture related chores of the families. The practice of veil was also not practised so strictly as it was in my paternal village and family. My *Naanee* I never saw in veil; she ventured out uninhibited, and contributed her mite to the agricultural pursuits of the big family alongside the male members. And I think, that was quite noble as well as sensible. Because of this freedom to venture out in the fields, their health – both physical and mental – was normally in fine fettle. Unlike that of the lady folks in our paternal hamlet!

As I have already mentioned, the area consisted of a cluster of three hamlets situated at hardly a distance of half a kilometre each; and people frequented all the three settlements as if the entire lot was one and the same village. The inhabitants didn't even harbour any feeling of being 'others' or 'strangers' while visiting the other units or settlements than their own one.

Our *Naanaa-Naanee* were quite often seen visiting the nearby hamlets called *Naglaa* and *Kathpuraa*, respectively; their own hamlet incidentally was called *Kunwarpur* – the settlement of princes. *Naglaa* literally meant a settlement, and *Kathpuraa* indeed meant the settlement built of woods, or set up inside the wilderness. Maybe at some time, in the fathomless womb of time, so to say, this small hamlet would have been set up within the wilderness or a jungle! Where they would have enunciated *Kathopanishad*, who knows! Whenever they – our *Naanaa-Naanee* or *Maamaajee* – passed or visited this way, we children loved to accompany them, too; for no specific purpose, of course; simply for having fun or simply for the sake of fun. For, passing through the hamlets or between the hamlets it always gave the feeling as if we were passing through a verdant pasture of nature's bounty. Such a fertile land! Such a dense vegetation all around it was!

How strong would the warriors – obviously our ancestors - have been who managed to capture these profusely fertile swathes of soil in the northern part of India? In the *Doaabaa* of rivers *Gangaa* and *Yamunaa!* They say, the land was trampled under the hoofs of horses of tyrant, marauder *Muslims* having come all the way from *Turkiye*, *Kaabul*, *Mangoliaa*, *et al*, then how is it that the entire land mass has still been under the occupation of our ancestors, our clansmen only? I oftentimes mused, and still do. Probably by ousting the occupants or shooing them away, or making them menial castes, the lower castes;

subjecting them to do servile duties, ever to remain wretched for life. Making them *Dalits!* That's all about the phenomenon of *Dalits,* as I contemplate!

This noble as well as meditative thinking apart, being the scions of such well off pedigree, we harboured in our childish hearts lot of arrogance and false pretences, no doubt. For we were accompanying our *Naanaa-Naanee* and at times *Maamaajee* too, they made the best of the opportunity and assigned us children some light tasks to be done, which at times we liked, but oftentimes, rather, mostly did dislike, especially, the tasks entailing manual labour. We were there for enjoyment! For having fun! Not for doing any errands of elders! I was particularly loath to do anything involving labour, for at my paternal set up it was an anathema to indulge in physical labour. Nonetheless, there was no exception for anybody here, I being a guest of honour notwithstanding. Now, when I look back, I feel heartily thankful to my maternal relatives for having inculcated in me some semblance of industriousness and laboriousness, which proved of utmost value as well as a key to success in my later life and career. The habit of exerting laboriously percolated down to my psyche and exhibited itself in all sorts of tasks later on: be they physical or be they mental, that is, official.

The man is a social animal, and through the agency or phenomenon of marriage, a man gets related to other strangers in what is called society; and in turn, an intricate cobweb of relationships gets woven. For, in my race or cast, whatever one might dub it, it was the practice to marry only within a specific circle, that was decided by applying so many norms of purity of genes and blood and *blah blah* that almost every next person within the caste or clan was found related by this or that way to oneself. Our *Naanaa-Naanee* or *Maamaa-Maamee* were no exceptions. They had their relations *inter alia* in these three settlements, too. And they visited these hamlets actually to see them off and on!

One such relationship of our maternal family was there in *Naglaa*: the family of *Yashodaa* who had a son named *Daamodar*. Perfectly matching nomenclatures: mother *Yashodaa* and son *Daamodar* – *Krishna*. And in my childish fancy I felt that this *Yashodaa* indeed resembled the *Yashodaa* of mythological renown, both in demeanour and in physique. More so, because our *Naanaa-Naanee* visited them as their saviours. The lady was a widow, and I have a hunch going by the patronising attitude of my maternal grandpa that her husband would have been a great friend of our *Naanaajee. Daamodar* at that age possibly having been quite a calf analogically to the cow *Yashodaa,* was under the constant protection of our *Naanaa*'s family and was very fond of them. Virtually they felt like being the members of this family only, of course, living at a short distance!

Another family which they visited was situated in the hamlet called *Kathpuraa.* And hold your heart, they visited the homestead of *Guddee*'s parents, to be precise! Their case was also almost similar to that of *Yashodaa* and *Daamodar.* Here, in fact, *Guddee's* mother was living in her paternal village, her parents having expired without any male heir; and *Guddee*'s father was the guest of honour for the village – a *Ghar Jamaaii.* He, in fact, hailed from some other village, of course, in the same district and the name of that village was *Nagariyaa.* Had he been living in *Naglaa* – the other hamlet – it would have been a poetic combination, with the inhabitant of *Nagariyaa* having migrated to *Nagraa*; nevertheless, he was living in *Kathpuraa.* Thereby depriving us of the poetic pleasure that we might have derived from this poetic symphony! He was gifted with an impressive personality, and also, with ample amount of social traits; and I felt, he was a good conversationist. Unlike *Guddee!* Who was a girl of few words!

Whom even this new lad had not had the courage to ever call by her name!

Whenever our grandparents proceeded towards this household, immediately I felt a queer sense of bewilderment and excitement within my body, for I could not bear to be in such a close company of my beloved sweet heart, *Guddee!* My countenance started taking a shape of buffoon and my heart started pounding heavily associating itself with a thunderstorm of feelings of love and romance, and sin having arisen in my whole existence. I never could comprehend this spontaneous as well as unbidden development in my body, nor could I ever control it. I, therefore, sought pretences to stay away or behind my grandparents, and would stop at some other homestead where I would find some or the other of my school-mates. One such schoolmate was the son of a tailor, and his house was in the alley leading to *Guddee*'s house; and I took shelter there, sitting on the cot outside his small hut or dwelling, my *Naanee* hailing me from afar notwithstanding. Thus I was saved of the awkwardness and bewilderment that could have arisen in me in the presence of my Lady Love – *Guddee*. Let me be very clear here that all this was merely on my part; the poor folk – *Guddee* – didn't have slightest inkling about all this buffoonery on my part. She didn't

possibly think anything about me! What sort of a weird mannered that lad – that's me -- was! An ape indeed!

In between these two dwellings that were located at the extremities of the two disparate hamlets, amidst the greenery and bounty of Nature, nestled in the fields, alongside the path leading from *Naglaa* to *Kathpuraa* there was yet another homestead, or to be precise, an assortment of thatched huts in a vast expanse of land. This was the house from which invariably, whenever our party was passing by, there emanated cries of excruciating pain and suffering from the throats of children. And hearing this, whether this were my *Naanaa, Naanee* or *Maamaa,* of whom the latter himself was quite harsh and strict towards children, whenever they passed by through this way and heard the excruciating cries, they could not help stopping and entering the hutment. To reprimand the lady who were found beating her innocent sons and daughters; and very cruelly, mercilessly! The innocent kids did cringe under the agony of physical suffering and pain being meted out at the hands of none other than their own mother: the same entity – the mother - who is proclaimed to be the epitome of love and affection towards one's issues!

This lady was a destitute, too, having been left alone after the demise of her parents in the village; and her simpleton husband having migrated to this village, the village of his wife. He was also a *Ghar Jamaaii*, alike *Guddee*'s father! He, incidentally, was the watchman at the level crossing of the railways that passed in between the gap of *Naglaa* and *Kathpuraa*. The squeaks and wailings of these kids were such that no passer-by could help entering the house and reprimanding the cruel and insensitive lady. What would have been the fate of that lady when these kids had come of age, I wonder. Would she still be expecting respect and good behaviour from those tortured lot of innocent toddlers, youngsters and teenagers. Preposterous preposition! In my considered opinion, she deserved the same treatment from the latter as did the kids get from her! Mental torture at least, if not physical thrashing!

My elders, relatives, rebuked the lady mockingly and derisively trying to make her see the cruelty she was raining upon her innocent kids. All of them were heard sighing: 'What a *Dusht* (devilish) woman you are! You don't have an iota of sensitivity towards children's pain and unbearable agony?....' This remark I had heard umpteen number of times invariably every time we passed by this assortment of huts from the mouth of my *Naanaajee,* from the mouth of my *Naanee,* from the mouth of my *Maamaajee* – who himself was not a lesser devil when it came to dealing with the kids – however he did not use physical force, he only wielded his rebuking tongue as lashes, and from the mouth of many others, like my mother – who never used physical force against me – such a lovely creature indeed she was!

XXX

16. Cotton Crop And Wealth Of My Mother

Enter Mother

One year is a pretty long period in the life of a young lass whose marriage had been solemnised only about a decade back or so; and who had been obliged albeit by circumstances or Providence to stay away from her young husband the whole year long. My parent's village was very rich in respect of Nature's bounty; its soil was extremely fertile. There was plenty of water resources available in the area, it being located in the delta of or the catchment area of – the land between -- *Gangaa* and *Yamunaa* rivers, both of which, were ever filled with water. Naturally, not an inch of the soil there was found without some vegetation or the other. Except, of course, the patches which had been covered by concrete in the name of human habitats, in turn, in the name of development!

For soil was fertile and families were small-sized by the standards of those olden days and the land holdings were quite large, the crops were sufficient to meet the requirements of one and all, and also, to spare, with the natural corollary that the temperaments of inhabitants were suave, sweet and jolly. They met one another invariably affectionately. There were no apparent signs of internecine rancour or envy, too, amongst the folks; lot of camaraderie was seen there.

All sorts of crops were grown by rotation following scientific norms of crop cycles by the farmers, like, maize or corn in the rainy season, wheat and barley in the winter season, of course, sugarcane round the year – which needed not be sown every year, rather, its shoots resuscitated themselves after every annual cutting, betraying the drama of perennial cycle of Creation which never stops unless *Nirvaan* is attained, that is, the cycle of reproduction (birth) and destruction (death) ceases!

Cotton was one such crop which was sown in the season of corn but continued long after the harvesting of corn had been done. Its bushes when its buds did start blooming did look like thousands of white stars in the sky. The cotton splitting out of the shells looked so pretty, precious and enchanting! Why only the cotton crop, during the flowering of cotton fields, even the sight of the field itself presented a mesmerising spectacle, that of a flower bed resplendent with variegated hues of flowers, on which did buzz the bumblebees, butterflies, and also, innumerable types of species which crept around, oblivious of the risks involved to their fragile bodies that could get crushed under the feet of humans who were by nature callous and insensitive towards their fellow brethren, particularly, in lower existences, or towards the other insignificant beings obtaining in the conscious creation.

For lots of water was available underground, and plenty of water was made available by the Government by way of canals and brooks in the area, there was no dearth of water and no difficulty in watering the crops that needed plenty of water. That may be exactly why the gods – particularly, the rain gods – were very munificent and favourably disposed towards the area; and when they willed to provide their bounty to the inhabitants, they provided so much that all the fields, crops, the banquettes and dividers did get submerged in the water. And in this anarchy, the wily peasants were seen devising methods to leak out their water to the side of others on the low lying areas, with the result that even those crops which were so far unharmed by rains did get submerged and destroyed. But such prodigal shows of Providence were far and few between and once in a while only, seemingly so as to set the arrogant heads of the human beings right. Mostly, the crops sailed through safely, to the relief of growers.

Whereas the cutting and disposing of the sugarcane crop was a lengthy as well as time taking process, and also, quite pleasing one, literally warm and full of glamour in the precincts of the crushers, the handling of cotton crop was in no way any lesser pleasing and interesting, too. For the land holdings of my parents and our close relatives were quite large, it was not easy to handle the vast tracts of fields of cotton crop single-handedly by our family members; it required the assistance of so many human hands. The cotton produce needed to be gleaned one by one from every flourishing bud. Nonetheless, it used to be a very interesting chore. Once in a while the menial workers – supposedly of lower strata of society who were called lower castes – were invoked and they came in dozens and droves. Moreover, the season at the time of harvesting of cotton produce would have turned the corner, the rains having stopped and salubrious warm season of early winter having set in. It used to be a dry season which was desirable, too, for safeguarding the produce as fragile and perishable as cotton. The ladies while gleaning the cotton from their shells did sing melodious folk songs and the tedious and dreary task became easier, even as, the task and time could not torture the workers, it passed off fairly unnoticed.

The system of compensating the labourers was in that they got a certain proportionate share of the cotton gleaned by them individually; a perfect and flawless system to encourage efficiency and its commensurate reward. Those who performed hard did get higher reward, and those who lacked efficiency did get lesser, of their own volition, no questions asked, or no grudges made. This practice was adopted in respect of all the crops where involvement of labourers' hands was warranted.

I being the member of the family almost permanently was obliged to help in all the chores concerning agriculture. Whatever cotton I gleaned, the entire lot was allotted to me; there was no taking away by my mother, or father, or brothers, for that matter. A special favouritism for the family member. I was able to gather a huge amount of cotton in this way that year. My mother told me that I could keep my share apart and when the cotton crop was taken to the market for selling, I could send my sacks separately for selling.

When finally, the huge amount of cotton crop was sent one day with lots of glee and fanfare by my relatives to the market, my share also did go in a separate sack. My mother especially mentioned this fact of my share to my son, as well. On hearing this, my son was happy and he expressed his pleasure to me, "Our share is also there in this riches, mother?"

In the evening when they returned from the market with faces resplendent with happiness, my father handed me Rs.30/- which was a huge sum by the standards of those times. I was so happy! I felt as if despite being away from my indolent husband – who had left me in lurch – I had become super rich overnight.

However, I could not keep my happiness to myself, to my bosom, and when my toddler son – who studied in the school – came running home, I took him to the room where my personal belongings were kept in a box. I took out the three new and crisp ten rupee notes from the folds of my clothes and showed them to my son. He apparently got very ebullient on seeing new, crisp notes and, particularly, those in the hands of his otherwise destitute mother!

'These are ours, *Beebee?*"

"Yes, these are ours!" I rejoindered with a tone that was a mixture of melancholy and glee. I also added, "My father has given me new crisp notes: these for you!" I beckoned towards the notes.

Nonetheless, I knew, these notes were nothing for that incorrigible indolent lad who was solemnised as my husband till the end of this life of mine or his. I knew that as soon as I would reach that haunted village, the fiend of that person would snatch away this huge sum and burn them within no time on his dissipated life! Even this money, the recompense of my labour was not going to remove his deliberate and self-imposed wretchedness!

XXX

17. Pedlars & Bade Naanaa

Enter Protagonist

Having all of us descended from the pedigree of *Raanaas* and *Raawals* of *Raajasthaan* and having mythological connections with the dynasty of *kshatriyas* of *Krishna,* the personalities and temperaments of the people in my maternal relatives' village were quite impressive; they looked like proverbial *Aaryans.* They had very strong longevity and lived up to a shade below one hundred years or so invariably. One may relate that directly to the better food and facilities, but that itself is proof enough that they were having influential and sturdy bodied persons as their ancestors.

Nonetheless, they were very pragmatic; and as an epitome of pragmatism was our elder *Naanaajee* – the elder cousin of our real *Naanaajee.* He had a very impressive personality and was seen always clad in very elegant dress, resembling *Rabindranath Tagore*, so to say, even as, he was tall as a stalwart and handsome alike *Tagore*. He may not have been as gifted in the realm of literature as *Tagore* was but he was commensurately gifted as regards the social skills required in that particular geographical area.

My mother was often heard complaining about him that he did not allow his granddaughter who was of my mother's age to venture out to play along with the children of her age. He was so suspicious of the social evils – read sexual mischiefs – to which the adolescent lasses might be easily susceptible, my mother commented. Whereas her own father, that is, my real *Naanaajee,* was not at all suspicious about such eventualities; he permitted my mother to go play and mix up with the lasses and lads freely; my mother had this impression. Nobody likes strictness even when it is imposed for the good and safety of the individual. My mother was a naughty, mischievous and sprightly sort of a creature in her childhood and adolescence. In

youth, of course, she could not afford to be, for she had been married with a hard hearted and insolent brat. Still I observed that she tried to retain her sense of humour even during her adulthood. Yet for how long! Ultimately the sapling of mirth and playfulness withered under the ever oppressive presence of her indolent and deranged husband who could not provide her even two morsels of food without having to worry about it.

This elder *Naanaajee* of ours not only kept a keen watch on the innocuous affairs of the lasses and lads of the hamlet, but also, kept a watchful eye on the workings and dealings of the pedlars and hawkers that frequented the village for selling their wares: vegetables, fruits, toys, ice-cream, *et al.* For it was a hamlet, cash was scarce; the only plausible mode of exchange was barter system: to exchange grains and cereals in lieu of whatever was being bought from the pedlars.

On such occasions, our elder *Naanaajee* invariably involved himself unbidden in the entire scene of trading, for he knew that it was not easy for the gullible kids or innocent village folks to decide the probable quantity of cereals to be exchanged for the wares or vegetables bought from the pedlar. Normally, whosoever came to the village for selling his or her wares or items did exchange the items for equal quantity of cereals in weight. Now I feel in hindsight that the cereals costing dearly were exchanged on equal terms with the vegetables and wares that cost pittance. The vendors were quite clever in that regard; they knew that it was very profitable to trade their wares in the villages, with the gullible guys.

The fact that I have discovered now was already in the mind of our elder *Naanaajee*. To avert cheating of villagers and children at the hands of pedlars he called the latter to his side, to sit beside his cot, and whatever transaction took place, it took place under the watchful eyes of our elder *Naanaajee*.

Nonetheless, how long could *Naanaajee* survive or live; the time came and he departed from the scene for ever! The illiterate villagers, however, clever they might claim themselves to be in their shallow wisdom, are not good at arithmetic; and whoever is not good at arithmetic or mathematics is susceptible to be cheated at the hands of swindlers and cheats. Also, at the hands of life itself! Therefore, instead of depending on the protection of saviours like our elder *Naanaajee*, they must resort to improving their arithmetical skills. Mathematics is the language of the universe and the alphabet of Creation!

XXX

18. Three Vows & Sensuality

Enter Protagonist

Back to school! From the precincts of village – which in colloquial terms they called *Madaiyaa*, the hutments! Every thing was hunky dory in school; at least for me! I was the star of school here also! Quite alike I was at the town school there at my paternal village! People praised me and held me in high esteem. Classmates and playmates respected me and were in awe of me, sort of. I was enjoying my fame and myself profusely. I had no idea at all, nonetheless, that I was a destitute and that I was living in an exile, away from my rightful dwelling, and also, that my mother was staying away from her husband for abnormally long and that all this was a pathetic situation. No idea at all! No question of bothering myself about such and other unbeknown phenomena!

My mother might be feeling the heat of angst against her stay no doubt; it's not easy to live in refuge, under the tutelage of someone else, related or unrelated. Irrespective of whether one is blood relation or not! The world, especially the social set up is a sham set up, based on assumed conditions which when put to test prove to be fickle and fragile. No relationship ever stands the scrutiny of stress test. However, at times, off and on, I could watch the drama of rancour and pique getting played in that household as well; and I feel my maternal grandfather and grandmother were bearing the brunt in this behalf – of keeping us at their homestead despite there being a husband already assigned to this lady – my young mother.

Anyway, I don't know what happened in that one year and how my mother was managing to live the life of celibacy yearlong, but I could observe her always busy with this or that chore of the household. She was not only doing the chores indoors, she used to do the chores that were supposed to be the preserves of only the male folks in our paternal area, our paternal village, like, going to agricultural fields just in the style of male members, and working there just like the latter, cutting fodder for the cattle, rearing the cattle, milking the cows and buffaloes, the milch cattle, warding off the birds from the crops such as corn and maize *et al.* My mother did all these chores. She also smeared the sprawling compounds and walls of the habitat and the dwelling places of cattle with *gobar*, the paste of cow-dung, so as to make them tidier and cleaner look wise. She was quite a lass at that time – a youthful one – full of mirth, sanguinity and a very high sense of humour. She somewhere in her heart was

harbouring the hope that her indolent as well as insolent husband would one day turn the corner and would take the responsibility of his household upon himself instead of thrusting the same upon his in-laws. She had great if only baseless faith in the sham fact that her husband was the only BA in the area at that time. However, this proved to be a mirage; the education imparted in schools and colleges has nothing to do with the inculcation of skills to meet the challenges as well as requirements of life and the abilities to live one's life comfortably. It rather demolishes whatever stock of skills and virtues one is endowed with *ab initio* for taking on the life.

Some of the lesser diplomatic souls even would venture to ask innocently of my *Naanee* whether everything was alright with the wedlock of my mother, to which my mother mirthfully reacted commenting, 'My husband has forsaken me!'

In those circumstances, I was having two of my female cousins almost of my age, living in the same household, members of the same family. Both of them were one grade above me, and by virtue of this fact, they were studying in the school at *Jaabil,* not in my school at *Naglaa Kath.* But it was a very happy relationship; the household was filled with good fortune, at least for us children. Innocence and ignorance is such a bliss! By that time there was no question of my acquaintance with what is called 'sin' in Bible, the forbidden apple of the garden of Eden.

Nevertheless, not all the classmates of mine were innocent and unblemished like me. One day while at school and the teacher being off our sight, *Vinod* entered into a chat with *Ramesh* – the same proverbial lad who had pledged to avenge me the first day in connection with the episode of thrashing of *Raamveer*. And they were not discussing gospels, rather, they set off discussing sex in hushed tones pretending to be avoiding the overhearing by girls, who were sitting hardly at a distance of two metres and I am sure, they were overhearing everything *Vinod* and *Ramesh* were indulged in discussing. The genesis of this sinful misdemeanour was in the fact that the mother of *Ramesh* had already eloped with someone to *Delhi* deserting her two sons, leaving them with their helpless father. Therefore, sex or sensuality was not an anathema or a taboo in their household. *Ramesh* seemed to be sexually active, too. His gestures even at school towards girls were not unoffending or childishly innocuous.

He was narrating an episode – right or wrong, nobody could vouchsafe – in which he had seduced a teenager girl of his village – the same village where the school was situated – by binding the girl with *tri-vaachaa* (three vows). What three *vaachaa*? That she would honour her word by chanting three times 'I shall honour my word - I shall give, I shall give, I shall give – whatever you ask for!' Entirely childish! And *Ramesh* is reported to have fucked the girl by binding her this way in her fetters of vows. How could anyone break the three vows? When even emperor *Dashrath* could not!

But everything sounds real in childhood, in the absence of any prior precedent or experience!

Vinod got impressed unassumingly and without straining his brain any further. He got a clue. A call to action! And the same day and date! Why delay!

He summoned courage and asked me to join forces with him in this 'holy' (!) task, the pioneering adventure in the arena of 'sin', the 'holiest sin' as per Bible. Being absolutely bawled over by the mesmerising mechanism effective just like a panacea and pushed by the sweet titillation of sensuality, I agreed to partake of the spree or orgy, so to say. In the agricultural fields profusely obtaining all around! In the rich overgrowth of crops all around! Where there was no question of anybody noticing us, too! And *Ramesh* had prior experience of this strategy's effectiveness and fool-proofness!

Thereafter the closing hours of the school felt like aeons were passing. Our target for the day and for latter days was the only girl from our hamlet who accompanied us to school every day - *Raameshwaree.* Not a very pretty, sexy or glamorous girl! Simply a simpleton, somewhat blackish countenanced. Still, who cares! Just for fun's sake!

Finally the hour of closing arrived and we rushed towards our hamlet slinging our satchels on our little shoulders. I rushed apace, unable to control my heart beats and not finding myself up to the task proposed. I assigned the entire task to *Vinod* and promised that if everything went as supposed I would share the exploits of the act. And I rushed towards home. I was scared, too, that the incident could turn out to be quite a failure and might lead to untoward incident and loss of face for us, too.

I therefore did not go home; I rather went to a tree of *Jaamun* which was standing at a stone's throw from our dwellings. And I scampered upon it and on to the loftiest twigs where the leaves were dense and where I could hide myself well. I waited there with bated breath. I was ruing the day and my foolishness to acquiesce with *Vinod's* proposal of making 'sin' with that blackie. Nonetheless, the act of sin

and sex is such a seductive proposition that even at the risk of losing everything in the pursuit one takes the plunge, and relishes it. Even the ancient *Rishis* (sages) could not help it!

My eyes were fixed on the path only. The school could be seen pretty clearly from there and almost entire path was discernible from my spot on the tree. I saw that though quite late, both *Vinod* and *Raameshwaree* were coming at a normal pace. They were also seen talking to each other, but nothing was there to suggest that they had indulged in the sinful activity. When they came beneath my tree, I stopped breathing, too, lest she should watch me and upbraid me, too. I was certain that she might have rebuked *Vinod* in befitting and acerbic tongue! I heard *Raameshwaree* gibbering and muttering something in angst. *Vinod,* however, was unperturbed at all. Maybe because he had done nothing and he could always contend that he was simply joking or, simply, that the girl was lying. He was also conscious somewhere in his heart that the girl would not gather courage to disclose this obscene and untellable incident to anybody so unabashedly.

By the mood of the girl I apprehended that she would go straight to my home and disclose the entire despicable episode to my mother. Already I had the blood of earlier incident of *Raamveer* on my hands; now this, yet another sinful act! What is this boy up to, this son of an indolent father, my mother would think, I mused! I kept on sitting in the tree for quite long. People of the village of various hues kept on coming and going beneath my tree, for the common path passed beneath it. I was straining my ears to do *reiki* about what had ultimately happened as a climax in this episode.

When for long there was no sign of anything unsavoury having happened in the hamlet, I came down from the tree with my satchel slung on the little shoulder, however, with a deep sense of shame in my heart. I took a vow never to indulge in any such affairs in future. Such affairs are extremely stressful, and may lead to so many intractable complications, I came to realise by this episode. And I thanked God that nothing irreversible and inexorable had eventually happened. Even on the part of my accomplice!

At home also, I did not notice anything abnormal, to my comfort.

Nevertheless, I kept on being apprehensive. And my misgivings came true two or three days later. The girl had brought the seductive incident to the notice of my cousin, the daughter of my younger *Maamaajee*. One day when I was having food at home sitting on the cot, my cousin started uttering in a mirthful and sadistic manner to my mother who was cooking *chapaatees* in the big kitchen, '*Buaajee,* shall I disclose to you something secret about *Arvind*?' And she smiled seductively, too. The Biblical sin is such a lovely affair that everybody wishes to relish it: whether by way of relating it or by way of enacting it!

I was shocked. My heart started throbbing fast. What now? The *karma* that I had not even done had come to catch up with me! I had merely contemplated indulging in a slight mischief and that, too, at psychic level only. For that small *akushal karm* (misdeed) also, so much punishment! So much embarrassment! However, my mother was a seasoned lady. She had seen the world and possibly the workings of libido in the society; she found nothing horrible in this trivial as well as childish activity done by two ignorant lads with an equally ignorant girl of the latter's age. Possibly she hushed up my cousin and she no longer proceeded with the relishable tale.

I felt extremely relieved, indeed, having been let off at the hands of Providence. I learnt a lot from this small episode and vowed never to have any truck with the ladyfolk in my life. Probably that is the base of my female sex phobia throughout my life, from school days till adulthood.

XXX

Table of Contents

19. Friend, His Sister & Snakes
Enter Protagonist

However sad and rampant might be the scourge of casteism in the countryside – not only now, but also, in the past – we the children had little idea about it and took little cognizance of this factor while dealing with our classmates. Caste *per se* was not reflected on the countenance of a person or a child, for that matter, nor did it have any specific significance. However loudly they might be pronouncing through the official records that there was differentiation between various castes, we observed that there was no differentiation between us on the lines of castes in the school or class.

I used to visit the dwellings of my friends off and on, especially, those who looked neat and clean, or those whose fathers were employed somewhere, or were in the Govt job, and were thus reckoned amongst the respectable strata of society despite themselves being of so-called 'lower castes'. My impression even at that young age was that not the caste but the financial condition and the employment status of a person decided the social stature of a person in society. Those who were or still are considered as lower castes are in fact those whose financial condition is pathetic. Who would respect a wretch?

One day I happened to visit the house of one of such of my classmates. I had pre-knowledge that he was not of my caste, rather, was of so-called 'lower caste', sort of 'untouchable' one. Despite that I accompanied him, for he was intelligent and was always attired very tidily as well as impeccably, not only dress-wise, but also, demeanour-wise. I sort of cherished his friendship. He had a little sister – school going one – and she was equally pretty. When I reached his house – his pretty and attractive sister in toe – it turned out to be a thatched hut, not a conventional house. I was shocked, yet could not help taking pity on their condition – those two siblings. At their house, at that moment, their mother was not present there; in fact nobody was present there. The hut was left as though it was an 'abandoned' one, and it was lying open as if it were a thoroughfare. The hut was clean in the sense that whatever could be cleaned and dusted had been done, but there was a lot which could not be helped, like the open sewage and the crude drainage. But open drainage is not an abnormal sight in Indian rural milieu. So I was not shocked at least in that behalf.

Instead, I was shocked to

learn that the hut and its surroundings were infested with the reptiles – snakes – and that the other day a snake was found crouched on the bed of the little sister. Merely the mention of the snake and the incident was enough to run a terrifying sensation down my spine. I became excessively attentive lest the snake should slither out any moment. Nonetheless, my friend and his sister did mention the incident with a pinch of humour and fun as if they were mentioning about some toy kept crouched on the bed.

'Didn't it bite you?' I could not help asking.

'It didn't; that's why I am still alive! Standing before you!' he rejoindered jocularly. His sister chuckled first and then even laughed explicitly. I felt some awkwardness, for I was a known persona of the school and a pupil of the eyes of other students including the girls. His sister seemed to be equally under my spell. Exactly that might be on her subconscious mind in accompanying us to their hut that day.

Whereas we were talking and bantering, I felt that she was self-conscious in my presence. No need to repeat that I was ever a soul who turned self-conscious in the presence of girls and female folks invariably. And this lass was pretty and attractive, on top of that! Who cares for caste? Caste did seem to me a stratagem contrived by wily people of human society to put a check on such unbidden love affairs or incidents of romance anywhere and everywhere!

Her brother was an innocent boy. She was throwing tantrums to draw attention of us both getting dejected at her neglect by us as though. When we felt that she was inconsolable as well as incorrigible, my friend accused her of being a fussy child and a cry-baby as she ever was as per her brother; and we made it back to the school.

Nevertheless, the entire seemingly innocuous episode left an indelible mark on my subconscious mind whereby I felt that the pretty girl despite being a loveable commodity was not getting her due simply because of two factors, both of which were beyond her control: first, the condition of her house, secondly, her declared 'lower' caste which could never be compatible with the declared 'upper' caste of the lad, that too, a gifted one, a prodigy, a rising star.

XXX

Table of Contents

20. Mother, Her Friends And The Swing

Enter Protagonist

Our elder *Naanaajee* was reported to be exercising strict control over the girls, it was the grudge of my mother who would be loving freedom, but she herself was subject to strict control by her family members beyond a certain limit.

My childhood impression was that my mother enjoyed the status of a virtual princess and had a clout unparalleled to any other lass in the village or the three adjacent hamlets. The added feather in her plumage was that she was very sharp witted and had a very high sense of humour. I have no hesitation in holding that both these attributes were the outcome of the robust financial and social condition of her family as well as parents. She sort of lorded over the girls and boys of her age, even after getting married.

On one *Shraavan* (July-August) month afternoon, when it was drizzling making the weather extremely festive and the environs perfectly verdant, my mother was invited by some girls of the village living on the flip side of the hamlet to come join them on the swing which they had slung on a branch of a big tree in the orchard nearby. Orchards were a speciality of that area; almost every landlord had an orchard at least, in which, trees and fruit trees of different species were grown. More than fruits, it served as a haven for shady respite during scorching summers, and also, were a source of natural enjoyment, for both kids and adults.

The girl who had hailed my mother to the festivity was equally bold, sprightly and dynamic just like my mother was. For the first time I felt that the other girl was treating my mother on equal terms, not that reverently as other girls or boys did her. There, while playing with those girls, my mother was not appearing that confident and overpowering or overlording. Rather, the host did give a feeling of competitiveness with my mother, as though another commoner were competing with a princess and, that too, with a sense of rancour and revenge. She seemed to have invited my mother with that explicit aim at heart, I felt in my childish assessment even at that time.

However, after only a few minutes, I heard my elder *Maamaajee,* and then my *Naanee,* call my mother back, I don't know why. Nonetheless, even at that age, I could sense the import of their tones as to suggest that they did not like my mother to play in the company of those girls. And it was reaffirmed all the more when the host girl exclaimed in perverse tone when my mother took leave of her, which implied somewhat like this: 'alright go, under the protection of your siblings!'

Therefore, depending on the social conditions and family atmosphere, the characters of persons are framed, formed and developed, especially, in regard to sex and sensuality. The affairs of girls and boys at that age are measured on the scale of their affairs in the discipline of sex and sensuality. Whereas some girls are bold in taking plunges and are not hesitant or shy, some others are not bold by nature, nor are they allowed to take a plunge in such spheres. All that depends on who is living under whom, and also, under what sort of circumstances.

From this episode my impression of my mother's invincibility and insuperability was shattered in that every person is effective and impressive only within a limited sphere and arena, particularly in one's own area of influence. Just like an electron which has its efficacy and energy only according to its specific orbit! Beyond its orbit it forsakes its energy and effectiveness. Amidst adversaries and strangers anybody would lose lustre and charm, however, effective one might feel oneself otherwise. One should, therefore, try to remain within one's sphere of influence if one wants to shine unceasingly and does not want to disillusion oneself regarding one's sham superiority!

XXX

21. Comfort And Calamity

Enter Protagonist

A railway track passed through the landscape of my *Nanihaal* – the busy track of Northern Railway, the *Howrah-Delhi*

track. Earlier it was a single track during my babyhood as I recollect vividly, but by the time I was constrained to pursue my schooling in standard fifth at my *Nanihaal*, it was a double track, still amply busy, with multitudes of trains, both passenger and freight, plying every day. For the original track would have been laid in the nineteenth century, the bridges built at that time to cover or cross the brooks, rivulets or rivers falling on the very lengthy way were mostly made from wooden beams, called *'gaarders'* (guarders), even as, the wood at that time would have been aplenty and cheap as well. But who knew that the circumstances would take a turn for the worse and the forest cover on Mother Earth would deplete so swiftly given the unbridled greed of humankind and, in turn, the wooden logs would be a very expensive and scarce resource. Moreover, the anachronistic logs laid there myopically keeping in mind their limited lifespan were now seen rotting, leading to the risk of the tracks giving way under the terrific jerks of the ever increasing speed of the running trains. To replace the logs or guarders on the bridges on the way was a very tricky task given the busy traffic running thereon. Even a small bridge on a narrow brook that fell on the way and carried merely the rainwaters during the season took months to repair or replace it. In the process, the trains had to be halted before the site and then these were allowed to pass at zero-some speed somehow.

One such *Puliyaa* – tiny bridge – was there in the vicinity of our *Nanihaal*. During this year it was under repair, and all the trains whether '*hi-fi*' or 'VIP' as we called them, and whom we saw passing by at superfast speeds earlier, to our amazement, now stopped there first and then only they restarted at crawling pace. Even the airconditioned trains, like, *Raajdhaanee* which, to us, was the supreme vessel on the tracks! During the repairing job, the spot of *Puliyaa* had assumed the status of a virtual place for picnicking for us curious children at least, and that too, without a *paisaa* having to be spent. Lot of activity went on there day in and day out. Lot of noise, too! And that was a matter of great joy for us children. We were, however, not aware that it was a temporary phenomenon only, and that it would pass too, soon. During those three or four months of hectic activity at that spot we could never have contemplated that the spot would be totally deserted after some time thereafter.

Also, this development had resulted in a great comfort for the people of the area. Their normal railway station – *Daanwar* - was at a distance of almost two kilometers

from our *Nanihaal,* and for some other villagers it was all the more distant. Now when this repair work was underway there was no need to exert and go to the far off railway station. For all the trains were halting there without any rhyme and reason, the needy commuters could board whichever train from this spot only and easily. One might wonder how the tickets were arranged. Let me clarify that in those days and in those rustic areas nobody bothered such things as procuring a genuine ticket or had any qualms about travelling without a ticket. Even the TTEs dreaded those rustic folks for reasons well known to them.

As for us, we too utilized the spot for boarding the trains on some occasions.

Everything was going fine when fatefully one afternoon the villagers noticed that a big train, a '*hi-fi*' train was halted just beside our *Nanihaal* for exceptionally longer duration. The hissing of the steam engine of the train was a constant reminder that there was something unusual afoot. When the villagers lost patience they proceeded towards the train. A feeling of gloom was looming all around. The passengers of the prestigious train were getting restive; they were hanging from the railings of the windows and the doors alike the curious apes and baboons. Some of them were also venturing towards the scene of activity. An accident had taken place, an unfortunate accident!

I also followed my maternal grandfather towards the train. We stood by at a safe distance from the train. However, everything could be heard from that distance. The spot where we were standing askance was the very place where my mother had one day been summoned by her lady friends for enjoying the swinging during the *Shraavan* month.

My *Naanaajee* got morose to learn of the incident, rather, mishap. I could not make out anything of the incident. I enquired of my *Naanaajee*, "What is the matter *Naanaajee*? What happened?"

He did not respond to my curious poser for reasons only well-known to himself. Nonetheless, some other villagers who had also assembled there, one of them obliged me in a hushed voice, "A young man's legs have come under the wheels of the train and cut away!"

"How?" I could not fathom the import of the information being a child only.

"He is from the nearby huts. He is employed in military. He had come during the holidays on *Eid* festival and was to return today. However, the trains did stop here regularly, and he thought that he could board the destined train from here. But the *Puliyaa* has almost been completed, and the trains do not stop in the same manner as they did in the past; they simply slow the speed, of late, and soon pick up. The young and youthful boy, a sprightly soldier as he was, tried to climb the seemingly slowly moving train, but unfortunately his smooth palms slipped on the railings of the train and in the struggle to balance himself his legs got pulled under the wheels. So sad!" sighed the harbinger of gloom.

"But why should the train stop?", I asked getting baffled, "and that, too, a *Raajdhaanee* express?"

"Howsoever prestigious a train might be when anything of this sort happens and comes to the notice of the driver and the guard, the train is obliged to stop and take care of the suffering party."

It was later known that the train had to be driven back one or two kilometers to reach the spot where the young man got amputated. We also came to know that the young man was a *muslim;* he was a suave and sociable personality. Incidentally, post the partition on communal lines, these wretched *muslims* – hardly three or four families possibly of the same lineage – were living beside a pavement amidst the barren fields far away from the human habitats where *Hindoos* dwelt comfortably. Even by seeing them and their huts, anybody could tell what their state of existence signified. Merely a subhuman existence! Partition had subjected a multitude of innocent humankind to such penuries and miseries!

And on top of that, this onslaught of divine powers: their bread-earner had been maimed! A slight carelessness and temptation to avoid walking up to the railway station had cost an entire life; a calamity had befallen!

People around me expressed optimism that the army would take care of the youth, who was their soldier. However, I doubted it even at that young age. I had a gumption that in this world nobody cared or bothered about a maimed, an invalid and incapacitated person, leave apart the Government or military. I might have developed such a notion on the basis of the fact that in our own case, even our own father was not bothering for our maintenance and necessaries of life. We were constrained to rely on the mercy of our maternal relatives. I wondered as to what the military would do with such an incapacitated as well as maimed man; they require superbly capable persons, persons full of stamina and strength.

Unfortunately, my misgivings proved to be forebodings. Later on, while passing through those huts after a gap of a few years – a decade or so -- I noticed that a person with legs amputated was sitting on the rope cot in the scorching heat of summer beside his huts and venting his ire on the poor, innocent family members who were themselves no lesser than amputated, if not literally, at least psychically. The youth had been discharged from the military unit and was totally resourceless presently. Instead of becoming a helping hand for his family, he had now become an unbearable burden on the unbearable lives of those sub-human species, the by-products of Partition post exodus of the British.

XXX

22. English Numbers Are Easier To Learn

Enter Protagonist

That boy of supposedly lower caste yet endowed with impressive personality and countenance was not my only friend in the *Naglaa Kath* school; being the star boy of the school I was the focal point for everybody's attention and attraction, be they boys or be they girls, at least I felt so in my childish fancies at that time. Some girls I liked and loved, but they did not know anything about it; and some girls liked and loved me, but I did not know anything about that; it was like that. I felt puffed up in my glory, in my intelligence; on the seventh sky as though, and as if I was going to stay there – at that pinnacle - for good. By that time I did not know that everything in this 'created' world is impermanent; now I do, when all that has changed and vanished inexorably, and seems simply as a dream world in hindsight.

One such friend – a boy – was the son of an inhabitant of that village who was intimately associated favourably with my *Naanaajee*'s family. His father was the pupil of the eye of my aunt – the elder sister of my mother. She was very fond of him, I felt. His father had also been to the city where my aunt stayed with her husband, in connection with the former's job. In my childish fancies, too, I could discern that there was something sweet at the subconscious level between those two souls. They were though quite frank in their dealings and interactions and there was everything unadulterated so far as conduct was concerned.

This man was a person of very refined tastes and demeanour. His sons and daughters were alike – refined and well-mannered like him only. His younger son studied with me in my class. He was always seen clad in impeccable dresses. I cherished his company and friendship despite myself being the most gifted child of the school. Some traits in other people attract everybody, even the gifted ones. Actually, the elder brother of this boy was studying in higher classes, in high school, possibly in *Jaabil* or somewhere else. He, therefore, had the advantage of the guidance of his elder brother in connection with the studies. Nonetheless, I was insuperable so far as studies at the school were concerned.

One day I was obliged to feel envious towards the skills of this boy. It so happened that he and I proceeded towards the level crossing of the railways for drinking water. The water hand pump was there only; in our school we did not have a water hand pump. And the watchman of the level crossing incidentally was the same simpleton who was the husband of that cruel woman who used to torture her issues mercilessly as narrated heretofore. He saw us and warned that the train was looming and we should keep off the track. We did. After the train had passed, we reached the hand pump and drank water; however, in the process, we set off chatting, and by some stroke of luck, we tended towards reciting English numbers, the digits.

It needs mention here that in our Primary schools, in those days, English was not taught; it started only from sixth grade. I did not know the English numbers or alphabet, for that matter. Of course, I knew English digits, the numbers, up to ten. My friend started chanting one, two, three….. *et al* and reached ten, I in toe. When he proceeded beyond ten, I was baffled finding myself at a loss. For the first time I felt that I could be defeated, too, in certain fields of learning. And that it was not necessary that one would be knowing everything despite one being a proclaimed intelligent guy in some of the subjects.

However, my friend was very kind and considerate just like his suave and civilized father. He clarified to me, sensing and seeing my embarrassment, that his elder brother was studying in higher classes and that his brother had guided him. He also explained to me that it was very easy to memorise the English numbers unlike *Hindee* numerals. He explained that upto ten, the numbers were to be learned and memorised; however, from ten to twenty, too, some effort was warranted for memorising them; but beyond twenty, it was quite a smooth sailing, with only thirty, forty, fifty etc to be learnt upto hundred; all the rest were formed by using one's common sense by suffixing one, two, three etc. to these terms. I was thrilled to learn that learning English was simpler than *Hindee*; thus far I was given the impression that English was something to be under awe of, and that it was always difficult to learn a language that was not our mother tongue.

Despite feeling sort of inferiority complex in the presence of my friend's wisdom, I thanked him and thought in my mind that a lot depended on how one was placed in social and familial set up. My friend had the advantage of his educated elder brother; however, I didn't have that advantage. I was actually not aware by that time that my paternal family was the reservoir of English learning and tongue in the entire geographical area back there. That realisation, nevertheless, dawned a year later when I reached my paternal village. At the same time I drew solace in the thought that my friend's elder brother would not have had the same advantage as my friend was enjoying, for his elder brother would not be having any elder brother to guide him.

XXX

23. *Saw And* Bhoodaa

Enter Protagonist

Being the guest of honour while living even in the house of such a relationship as that of a father and a mother is no guarantee that one would command respect among the permanent inhabitants of the household. My mother and I along with my younger sister and a sister in her lap were staying there as already narrated. Though no obvious resentment or dislike was exhibited towards us by the inhabitants there, or maybe we being ignorant and innocent yet, did not have the faculty to feel the pain of such subtle humiliations, now in the hindsight, I feel that my mother would be feeling that pain of humiliation constantly.

For now I contemplate that the demeanour of my elder *Maamaajee* towards my mother was invariably harsh and cruel; whenever he commanded my mother, it was in a tone of utter cruelty. My mother was commanded to do the chores of the family which were the sole preserve of the male members as per the social conventions. I observed that the lady folks of the household never did engage in such chores as was my mother commanded to indulge in. She would be doing all sorts of outdoor duties and tasks in the agricultural fields and would be seen rearing the cattle, too. Still she was always at the receiving end of my elder *Maamaa*'s ire. In utter frustration, my mother sometimes was seen grumbling 'He is such a wicked person, a daemon! ' and I used to feel it myself. I myself was not spared, too. I was subjected to both physical labour on the fields and mental humiliation at drop of a hat. I kept on cursing him whenever he tortured my psyche by his bad behaviour.

He was fond of disrupting our childish games and would command some errand to be done. He proclaimed, too, that I was an indolent chap just like my father. This appellation was ascribed to me by many of the inhabitants of the household in my *Nanihaal,* but never

by my maternal grandpa. However, the latter – my *Naanaajee* - was always in an unsavoury mood whenever it came to mentioning the name of my father. He seemed to rue the day when he had decided to marry his daughter – my mother – with that brat, as though.

Seasons come and go, of which, some are salubrious and some very murky. And a year's time is quite a lengthy tenure. So many things happen over the period of a year. Likewise, the moods of the people see so many seasons and undergo so many variations. Agriculturists whose life depends entirely on the outcome of the agricultural activities also see the coming and going of variegated moods. They do so many things of different types over the year. And I was witness to all those phenomena during that one year of our stay at our *Nanihaal.*

On one such fine afternoon, when my *Maamaajee* had summoned a carpenter to do some sawing - to saw a big wooden log - and was himself associated with him in the tiresome and monotonous task of sawing the log by hand, the big saw they were using gave way and broke off in the middle. That was a big setback in the otherwise smoothly running affair. They grunted at this mishap, both my maternal uncle and the carpenter, or the master and the labourer, whatever you call them or love to call them.

Now, what to do? The entire envisaged plan had abruptly come to a standstill. I in my fancy contemplated, instead, that with the breaking of the saw the task that was at their hand had naturally come to a stop, with no further venturing about, or devising something anew. What a childish fancy, having no truck with the absurdities of the human world!

Nevertheless, this was not to be so; a peasant, or a labourer never gives up. With one setback on, he switches on to yet another conjecture and seeks recourse to some other person. They sighted me playing thereabout. I was in fact watching them at work, seeing the big log getting ruptured in the middle with the instrumentality of the saw, and was expecting to feel the thrill when the solid big log would fall apart in two parts. But they sighted me, and contrary to my conception that they would not involve me in their next conjecture, they ordered me to go to the nearby village, *Bhoodaa,* almost 2 kms away, beyond the brook and the dense orchard in between, and fetch a saw, begging the same from the friendly farmer of our *Maamaajee's* acquaintances. I grumbled and showed hesitation, first, for I took it as a high-handedness on the part of adults to instruct an unconcerned teenager to do their chores;

secondly, because I felt that the unknown villager who did know nothing about my identity would never give me the desired saw. I was an unknown persona for that farmer, however, friendly he might be to my *Maamaajee* or *Naanaajee.*

With a heavy heart and with weary steps I tramped towards the destined village, slowly and deliberately very slowly as if to avenge myself against those two adults, despite their clearcut commands that I should hurry up. I reached the destination and was sincere in my intent in asking for the saw from the owner of the house there, but as I was suspecting, they did not recognise me, or did not think me worthy of carrying a big saw on my shoulders, and they flatly, rather callously, declined to give me the saw. Instead of feeling disheartened, I felt glad that they had declined my request and that, as a result, I would not have to carry the burdensome saw on my shoulders.

On the return journey, as well, my steps were deliberately trying to delay the approach to the village. On the way, there was the brook full of water and seemingly seductive, too, for a child of ten. On the bridge of the brook, I could not resist the temptation of wetting my feet in the cool stream of the brook. When I was relishing this reverie of nature and administration jointly mixed up, no sooner had I wetted my feet than the carpenter happened to come that way. When he saw me sitting there and enjoying myself unconcerned about the important task at hand, he got very angry, and I felt, that he was angry unreasonably. He accused me of never having reached the village and having asked the owner for a saw, however hard I tried to clarify my position. His eyes were burning with rage as if this was me who had broken their saw and as if this was me who was the cause of all the malaise there was in their lives, the lives of adults! My truth, rather, the truth of the incident was falsified, I saw vividly; I was taken as a liar!

I got frightened, yet I did not think that there was any fault on my part. I waited there till the carpenter had reached the other village and had come back with the saw on his shoulder. Then I too followed him in toe, he gibbering and muttering all sorts of names for me: 'a brat, a careless and ungrateful brat!' *et al.*

On reaching the village he narrated the tale of my callousness and carelessness and enjoyment at the brook with added flavours. He also told them that I had never reached the village, rather, I was still sitting at the bridge of the brook making merry of myself. All falsehood being proffered as a truth!

My *Maamaajee* found a ready excuse for rebuking me, to my consternation. Where was I at fault? The villager did not give me the saw, what was my fault? The entire punishment that was being meted out to me was based on the falsehood and assumptions of the labourer. Not only *Maamaajee*, but also, my *Naanaajee* and *Naanee* upbraided me remorselessly. It was a very unique saddening experience for me. One could be upbraided even on the basis of falsified allegations, or assumptions. Whither the phenomenon of cause and effect in all this occurrence which is vouched so emphatically in this Creation?

However, this episode taught me that the relations that were however close were not free from usual rancour when one was obliged to live as a burden over them, as parasite. Parasites we were! Not for our own fault, but for the fault of our begetter! And the latter was least remorseful! Least concerned!

XXX

24. Eat To Your Fill, Lad!
Enter Protagonist

The episode of saw whereby my indolence was tried to be proved and established was not the only episode which showed how intriguing it is to keep one's issues at a relative's place. My maternal grandparents might not be minding our stay there but now in hindsight I feel that my elder maternal uncle did mind it and, as was his wont, always to be in an irascible frame of mind, he did not try to hide his annoyance towards us – his sister and her issues. Now I feel that the food there used to be very nominal: *chapaatees* and the pulses of peas mostly. If someone asks me now to eat the pulses of peas I may not like it, but at that juncture as well we kids did not like the pulses of peas. Actually, my maternal relatives were dependent wholly on the agricultural produce, and whatever they produced profusely they made their family members to consume that predominantly.

The only deviation in those drab routines of the villagers used to be when someone – old one or young one - condescended to die! For, post his or her demise, there was sure to be a sumptuous feast, thrown to one and all of the gentry in the entire area. The only good and interesting thing – also acting as a sedative, I think – in the entire phenomenon of 'dying' was the feast thrown after the death – thirteen days after the death; it was called *Terahveen*. Those whose loved ones died might be mourning the demise however mournfully, but for others including the kids like us it used to be an unbidden boon: a feast, in the preparation of which, not a trace of the sorrow in the wake of the death remained.

It was not necessary that one should die in one's own village for the purpose of availing the sumptuous feast, one could die anywhere in the catchment area of the village – miles apart from there – where the inhabitants belonging to the same clan or race or caste or profession, to be precise, dwelt. Caste is nothing but the same profession or vocation only!

On one such fortunate occasion, my maternal uncle took me along to *Jaabil* – a nearby village - for partaking of the feast on death – the *Terahveen* of someone. The invitation had been received almost a week back, and on the appointed date I observed that *Maamaajee* instructed the lady folks of the household to exclude himself and me from the day's roster of eatery of the household. He meant to convey that, for making the most of the occasion, we the duo who were to partake of the feast should be properly famished so that when we were served the items of the feast, we could eat to our maximum capacity, rather above our normal capacity: 'the more the better'. I was shocked; it was against whatever I knew and had learnt about food and diet so far. At my paternal village, they used to preach abstemiousness and frugality in eating; they preached 'the lesser the better'. Here, my maternal uncle was preaching just the opposite: 'eat more, eat more: the more, the better!' Also, in our school books, they suggested for eating the least. I could not understand the psychology of my maternal uncle. My common sense too suggested that in the matters of eating, the lesser the better!

My *Maamaajee* was given the fake epithet of a *'Swaamee'*, a saint, a hermit. Whither *swaamee!* He was of the considered opinion that if the opportunity arose to eat at the cost of someone else – even in the wake of someone's death – one must avenge oneself for the overeating done by the deceased or his or her relatives when it was the feast arranged by us on the occasion of our deceased ones. Thus, it was sort of a war: war of eating another's food, more and more!

I accompanied my maternal uncle to *Jaabil* despite my disinclination to have feast of any sort. Nonetheless, *Maamaajee* insisted that it would tantamount to us losing a platinum opportunity to harm our enemy by not eating his food at his cost. After all how much could a single person – *Maamaajee* – eat unless I – a youth – accompanied him to help in the war of eating! Despite his 'sermons on the mount' I had decided – and thought it innocuous – to not indulge in overeating, even as I thought it uncivil to overeat; rather, I thought that if I desisted from eating too

much, people there would praise me in their hearts: 'look, how little one eats!' This was my line of thinking! However, that was not my maternal uncle's line of thinking!

The feast was a big feast involving a large number of invitees – the supposed mourners – from all the villages around. First, we were made to wait in a hall – *chaupaal* – where other elders were assembled, waiting for their turns. They were not mourning the death of whoever had died thirteen days ago, rather, they were indulged in all sorts of socio-political polemics and rancorous chats. It showed how effective this system of feasting on someone's death was in abetting the pain of someone's death and in forgetting the one who had died!

My *maamaajee* was not a person who could not mingle with the medley of crowd. He started participating in the polemics of the elders uninhibitedly. His refrain at the beginning of every new sentence used to be *'Thaakuro!....* do this or do that....'. For instance, whenever someone complained that one felt weak in the old age whereas in the youth one was quite sprightly, my *maamaajee* would chip in , *'Thaakuro! Gheo khaao gheo!......'* (Martial races! Eat refined butter, eat refined butter!) *et al.* Or when it came to the huge expenses to be incurred on constructing a house, especially, a pucca house, *maamaajee* would chip in, spreading his *kurtaa's* lapel in front of one and all, '*Thaakuro!* It takes a lapel full of money many times to build a house, especially a pucca house!' *et al.* The audience, however, did not seem to be too much impressed by my maternal uncle's intrusions in the discourses, I felt. The reason for this in my child's contemplation might be that my uncle looked entirely rustic, a vulgar villager, however prosperous and pedigreed he might be. From this phenomenon, I drew the conclusion that outer appearance is equally important to command respect amongst strangers, particularly, villagers!

Meaningless *Chaupaal* discourses apart, the turn came soon for our feasting. And I failed my uncle at the feast. I showed at the feast that I was an abstemious lad. I considered that demeanour of mine as a virtue, a merit. Nevertheless, my *maamaa* didn't; more so, when he had already tutored me about the likeability of overeating. He hinted towards me during the feast, but to no avail. He asked those serving to give me the *poorees* and *kachaurees* and what not, but every time I forbade the servers, for I could not stand the sight of eatables. The feast ended somehow, to my reprieve. I heaved a sigh of relief.

However, relief it was no more for me on the way back home. As soon as we stepped on the pavement to our hamlet from *Jaabil*, *maamaajee* set off chiding me, muttering and gibbering about my disobedience and incivility in not overeating at the feast. He also accused me, deriding that I ate too much at home when it was at the cost of his own household, whereas today when it was to the cost of someone else I had eaten so little, thereby wasting the platinum opportunity of eating outside. He also predicted that I would eat again when I went back home for compensating for my not having eaten to my fill at the feast. All along that two and a half kilometre long stretch of the journey through wilderness or the agricultural verdure, I had to endure the irrational wrangling of my maternal uncle who was an adult of not less than fifty at that juncture. I despite being a child was wondering how foolhardy the adults could be! In the process, however, I recalled or missed my paternal set up where they never insisted for overeating, neither at home, nor at the feasts. They always preached abstemious eating for keeping healthy and fit.

In this behalf both the sides had their share of merits and demerits! My paternal side and maternal side!

Maamaajee did not stop there: he carried the complaint against my offence to the village and lodged it with everybody whoever came his way, including the village elders, *Pandits*, other uncles, my *Naanaajee et al.* And I kept on wondering! To my relief however nobody took this seriously, nor did anybody flog or upbraid me for my crime of not overeating.

So seemingly sane adults, or proclaimed *swaamees* may also be insane and depraved by demeanour; please beware!

XXX

Table of Contents

25. Vidyaa Dadaati Vinayam! *(Education Must Lead To Modesty!)*

Enter Protagonist

Childish behaviour in childhood is a common fallacy, for the child does not realise his folly; how could one? I being a gifted child and a pampered one, was full of arrogance concerning my exceptionality. This giftedness or superiority was a creation or boon of God, I did not realise this at that juncture. Now I realise that there was no specific contribution of mine in the phenomenon of my brain being sharp, or I being an intelligent student. It was so, of its own! Nevertheless, how could a child be capable of comprehending such subtle nuances?

I was able to do all the sums of the arithmetic book; I was able to read the vernacular booklet eloquently, and even to write it properly as well as correctly. Also, I felt erroneously that I was privileged to possess that intelligence exclusively for my own sake, that is, to the exclusion of others; and that no other chap should have the right to learn anything that I knew. Competition! Competition is such a demeaning vice! Teachers encourage it, English system of education encourages competition amongst students! Nonetheless, it's a very nefarious concept; it engenders ill-will amongst the impressionable hearts of children. I had experienced it in my previous school – in town; I did experience it here, as well. Therefore, by now I had myself developed this vice in the mutated form of selfishness: a tendency not to share any knowledge with anybody. Being on top in the class or school, I was always apprehensive and worried about losing my lofty stature in the class or school; and that stature could be preserved only by depriving others the benefit of my knowledge, I presumed in my childish folly.

Moreover, I had the arrogance that it was only me who could solve certain problems in the book of arithmetic. As though I was some prodigy, as if I was created especially for the purpose by the creator!

I did not help my classmates solve the intractable problems of arithmetic so as to remain the only student who could solve those questions. I did not help even my cousin *Vinod* – the same accomplice who designed that failed sexual experimental adventure with *Raameshwaree*. *Vinod*'s cousin – son of his elder uncle – was a teacher in a Junior High school in some town somewhere near *Delhi*. On one occasion when his cousin happened to visit the village, *Vinod* decided to take his help to get those sums done. However, his uncle could not solve those problems, to my perverse pleasure, as if ignorance of his elder cousin who was a teacher, and my exclusive skilfulness in solving the question, were a living testimony to my exclusivity and superiority in the arena of learning! His cousin asked me modestly as to how the question was to be solved. I refused arrogantly and proudly.

First he thought that I was just kidding, but when despite his repeated entreaties I did not budge, he became somewhat angry and commented, '*Laalaa* (Dear child!), so much arrogance is not good for life!'

My *Naanaajee* was sitting beside on a cot – a straw cot - and he took exception to my attitude of arrogance and self-centredness. He suggested to me that my demeanour was unworthy of an intelligent student, also that the wisdom and skills do flourish with every instance of sharing the same with others, implying thereby, the more one shares one's knowledge and skills with others the more one becomes intelligent. However, I was not to budge, as if the skill to solve those specific problems was my exclusive preserve, the gem or the diamond, which I could not afford to part with.

When I did not help them, my cousin – daughter of my elder *Maamaajee* – who was playing there chastised me in these words, "Why don't you tell and solve the question? Why are you so arrogant? You are so insolent as to disrespect even such an elder as our cousin, a teacher; shame on you!...." She kept on saying so many things but to no avail. I was not wise enough to understand all those lofty ideals at that juncture in my life. I surmised at that juncture as if self-centredness and meanness were the only virtues to be possessed in life! I did not share my knowledge with them. How possessive I was, I now realise! How wrong I was, I reminisce with a sense of extreme regret presently! Especially, later when I read the *Sanskrit* idiom *'Vidyaa Dadaati Vinayam!'* (The education must lead to humility and magnanimity!)

XXX

26. Childish Shopkeeping
Enter Protagonist

Because the dwelling units of our relatives were very spacious and sprawling, there was scope for doing many things childish as well as creative. On one side of the big house there was an entire field left vacant, in which, there were growing several types of trees, and also, some vegetables were grown there. And I was the main *Maalee* (vegetable grower or green grocer, so to say) of these vegetables there.

However, I was not content with only growing vegetables. I launched a new project, that of opening a shop through which I intended to sell wares of the interest of children. Agriculture is alright but one must diversify into some commercial pursuits also for becoming rich! The era was that of commerce, the agriculture pursuits were losing sheen day by day, as I realised in my childish psyche.

Therefore, I decided to first erect a shop beside the wall of the house - for the sake of safety and security of the shop. I started building the *kutcha* shop by raising the walls with the help of muddy clay. Daily I raised the wall to some height and then let it remain like that for drying and seasoning, and then again I raised it somewhat more, and then left it to remain for drying in the sunshine. This way it took quite long, but there was no dearth of patience on my part, nor any dearth of time. A year seemed to be quite a long period, not less than an aeon for the child's psyche and perspective!

Ultimately the shop was ready, the walls had been erected, and enough to cover me if I sat in the shop and if there was a roof over it. Then the roofing was the next big issue; how to arrange it? I took help of my mother and *Naanee* in this behalf; they suggested and helped me acquire some tender sticks of heather from the thicket and some mud, and the roof was finally laid and was ready. When it got dried up properly, I invited the who's who of the household to come see the spectacle I had created in the form of a commercial complex just beside the big house where merchandise of all sorts would be sold in immediate future!

The elders merely laughed off, yet did not discourage me by condescending to enlighten me that it was not that simple to run a commercial complex or a shop: who would supply the stock of merchandise and who would buy them? It turned out likewise eventually. I was depending on my maternal cousin – *Surendradaa* who stayed in *Aleegarh* with his father for study – for supply of saleable stocks. He, however, brought at least once the merchandise in the form of some toffees and sweet globules etc. in a jar of glass, and I sat with that jar inside the shop along with *Daadaa*, waited patiently for the customers to come; but ultimately came none. We tried to seduce the family members to purchase our wares/ fritters but nobody helped, except laughing innocuously.

Ultimately we realised that our dream-world was sham, it had no element of hard reality; it was not necessary that it would work. The real world may be called *Maayaa* – delusion – but this delusion has a lot of materiality in it, to cope with!

XXX

27. Buaa's Marriage At Village
Enter Protagonist

I had a *Buaa* - the younger daughter of my father; of course, she was the youngest one of the four destitute children left after the untimely demise of their young mother. Having been brought up in the absence or in the wake of the death of her mother, she could not develop her faculties as properly as a normal child would have developed; she was considered to be a simpleton, a demi-deranged personality which, I vouch, she was not. She was simply a simpleton, and kind-hearted lady. Somewhat irritable, irascible, and having only a modicum of sense of humour. People made fun of her, no doubt, and she invariably took exception to peoples' umbrage.

This aunt of ours was not the only one to have been stunted in mental growth; my own father, who was only slightly elder to her, had also developed the same sort of tantrums as this aunt had. My assessment is that after the death of their young mother, their elder aunt – *Badee Ammaa* – having been burdened by this extra load of the latter's issues could not bring herself up to treating the little kids sympathetically at the subconscious level. Her demeanour towards these destitute children would have been that of contempt and humiliation. It is self-evident from the fact that *Badee Ammaa's* own children did not develop any such tantrums, traits or quirks, whatever one would like to call them, as my father and aunt had developed.

For our real grandmother had died, there was a desperation amongst the family elders and well-wishers of the family to somehow arrange marriages of the children so that their households could become self-dependent and come out of the clutches of *Badee Ammaa;* nonetheless, I had never heard a word of complaint from the mouths of my father or the aunt against their elder aunt. This conundrum I have never been able to fathom.

My elder aunt – the elder sister of the same lady – however, was heard making a stray remark once in a while that their uncle – the husband of *Badee Ammaa, Netaajee* – did not care much about the well-being of them while arranging the marriages of the latter; he arranged the weddings keeping in mind the wealth and pelf of the families of bridegrooms or the brides than the worth or countenance of them. One testimony of which was that the husband of my elder aunt – *Buaa* - was of dark complexion unlike herself who was fair complexioned. This might have worked on the subconscious mind of hers while making this remark, I thought.

Also, not directly criticising his uncle – *Netaajee*, my father was heard making almost the similar allegation against his saviour when he sighed while narrating his tale of marriage in the agricultural field while weeding the millet crop there. He had commented with a sense of wonder where his dowry money – huge sum of one thousand sovereigns in gold – had gone, whereas he had been saddled with a liability in the form of a young lady, and also, his educational prospects had been marred for good. Nevertheless, I had combined together the two complaints made by both the siblings - sister and brother - made at disparate spots and times that the wily old man – *Netaajee* - might have used the money thus earned to arrange marriages of his own issues and daughters in good households and with prospective bridegrooms, which they indeed were, better ones in comparison to those of our aunt – *Buaa* - and father.

Netaajee had long died however, and now it was up to my grandfather's own family to take the load of family, livelihood, and also, the marriages. And for that matter, my elder uncle – *Taujee* – was there. He had been married long back and was considered to be a sane and seasoned person unlike my own father, who was considered to be a certified deranged persona.

To cut the long story short, my *Buaajee* stayed with my elder uncle and aunt. My father had no wherewithal, it was true, too; nor did he feel any qualms of conscience in such regards. My elder uncle did. Likewise, my grandfather stayed with elder uncle too; and he was an indifferent sort of personage. The English education had rendered him as though totally inactive and indolent; he did not like to use his hands and brains on any worldly chores. As if 'educated' meant 'good for nothing', a 'worthless fellow'! He did not care for agriculture, he did not care for doing any service or job, he did not assume any responsibility of household, even as, his wife had died. And it is rumoured that she died exactly for this reason: in that he did not take upon himself any responsibility whatsoever of running the household; every chore was to be done by my grandmother, it is rumoured, and it was under the weight of those gruelling liabilities that she finally succumbed to the ultimate saviour, the death, one day, ridding herself of all miseries of a married life, and of life itself!

While living in the Elysium of my *Nanihaal*, we heard the news that our *Buaa* was due for marriage soon. It came as a saddening news for me, for *Buaa* was a very affectionate personality for us kids – the children of her brothers. We had never assumed that there would come a day when she would no more be the member of our household; we in our childish fancies were considering her as a permanent fixture of our paternal household. It was not so; like everything else, that was to change, and that change was imminent.

On my expressing shock at the news, my mother expounded to me that the same was the fate of every girl, and that *Buaajee* would no more be found at our paternal village. Oh so saddening! I mused.

We made it to our village, of course, with the instrumentality of the company of *Modhoo chaachaajee*. In our life's journey, *Modhoo Chaachaa* was a crucial link, as if to act as a saviour or as a sailor of our hindered journeys, father being an indifferent entity, not taking any active part in the journeys of our lives.

At our village, for we did not have any homestead of our own, we somehow managed to stay in the same ramshackle *kutcha* enclosure of *kutcha* walls with semi-covered or semi-bared roof, whatever one might dub it. I felt so depressed having reached that house, coming as we did from such a sprawling and spacious house of our *Naanaajee*. We were respectable entities there, but here nobody cared for us. For my father's contribution was little in arranging the marriage of his younger sister, there was no sense of obligation towards his family on the part of our elder aunt or elder uncle. Moreover, under the influence of her elder sister – who was the wife of the eldest uncle in the household – my mother behaved adversely as well as maliciously towards my real aunt - *Taai*, who was an educated and progressive lady, my mother being an illiterate one with the burden of so many superstitious beliefs, whereas my aunt – *taai* --did not harbour any; she rejected all dogma and bad rituals, and sensibly so.

Marriage got solemnised eventually, but I was disheartened, for our say in that whole affair was little or none. Also, I felt that we were being treated as mere non-entities in the entire episode. Our elder aunt – *Taai* - was not paying any attention to us. This was a very depressing prospect. I inferred from this journey, and from experiences derived therefrom, that my father was a non-entity – a naught -- in the whole scheme of things of the household; and that I was the son of a person who was not a father figure or fatherly stuff at all. I had nothing to sing home about as regards my father! My mother, on the other hand, who looked so effective and energetic in her father's home, here looked like a pale personality as though moribund, as though living in the *harem* of a warlord: with no respect, with no self-esteem at all. How much difference can the circumstances make to a living being's personality and behaviour!

Nonetheless, despite my uncle's and aunt's indifference and neglect of ours, one soul at least was there who was quite warm towards us; this was my cousin – the younger son of my elder aunt – *Yuvraaj*. He was very kind, considerate and behaved like a noble soul, in a sense. Extremely affectionate! On the day of marriage party's arrival, he took me along and we collaborated with other persons who were decorating the places for stay and arrival of the marriage party.

In the evening, when the marriage party arrived, my cousin held my finger, and we both dared to reach the bridegroom where he was seated in the big hall on our *khedaa*. Our *foofaajee* – the bridegroom – was the owner of very impressive personality and health. He was very handsome as well; and I was wondering how these people of feudal lineage could arrange to marry such a handsome and gifted lad with a simpleton lass like my *Buaajee* who was no match at all for the bridegroom. She was not at all a match for this handsome lad, in a sense, it seemed to me as a perfect treachery with the married life of a promising youth. Nevertheless, that is exactly what feudalism is all about! In the era of princes, princesses and princely states, myriad such unwelcome developments took place in the name of marriage of any Tom, Dick and Harry being contrived with any other Tom, Dick and Harry pronouncing them as princes and princesses, whereas in actuality those were merely the issues of the black countenanced slaves and maid-servants of the real royals, however, impregnated by the latter.

Living up to the tantrums of the feudal families, there took place many arguments and squabbles between the two sides during the marriage ceremony, like, the uncle of the bridegroom raised the issue of dowry whereby as per his version a watch was, *inter alia*, to be gifted to the bridegroom, which was not done. And it turned out incidentally that the villain in this episode too was my father only as ever; he was reported to have promised the other side during his visit to them somewhat prior to marriage ceremony that they would gift a watch, and also, other such trifling items. However, like a callous chap, he consented to everything and did not even convey this matter to his elder brother who in fact was arranging everything. There was lot of hue and cry, and my father was blamed for his madness as he ever was. My elder *foofaajee* who was from the area of the bridegroom only declared with firm conviction that my father was a confirmed madman, not only a madman called jocularly. My father was, however, characteristically little concerned about all this; he could not realise the gravity of his unconscious promises made unattentively at such a crucial occasion as a wedding proposal!

XXX

28. *Loss Of Face For A Coloured Jackal*

Enter Father

In the millet field where we were weeding the crop along with my elder son, when I had finished the story of my *Veerpuraa* stay, and of fleeing from there having embezzled two hundred rupees from the school, my son asked me about my tenure at *Jhaajhar* school. So far I was posing myself there – at *Jhaajhar* school - as a prince, the scion of a very wealthy and influential pedigree. Resultantly, the teachers and the management were all under my awe. They respected me like a prince, or a bully only! In absolute terms, both are synonymous!

However, during my younger sister's marriage, I was obliged to invite all of them to the marriage party. They were expecting a warm welcome there. But my sister-in-law did not care for them, nor did my elder brother; for both of them they were unnecessary burdens or avoidable nuisances, having come there to have feast. They did not offer them anything even to eat, not to talk of feasting. All of them had come thinking that this was the marriage of a respectable family – a 'big' family as they called it - and it was their duty to pay attendance there.

It turned out to be a damp squib incidentally. The facade erected on the basis of falsehood and hypocrisy came crashing down! It so happened as if the jackal in coloured skin had ultimately been identified by the beasts of the jungle! The teachers could realise to their chagrin and derision that I commanded no respect in my family. And that was true, too. By habits I was an indolent lad, contributing nothing to the family; how could I then invite so many extra mouths for partaking of the feast which was being offered by someone else, irrespective of the fact that this was my sister's marriage.

My son enquired about the tussle having erupted during the marriage party and the bad blood having developed between my elder brother and the bridegroom's uncle. I explained that during my visit to the village of the bridegroom, the latter had asked me to convey some messages to my elder brother concerning gifting of some specific items as dowry; or maybe they thought that I being the younger brother might be having some sense of responsibility in the whole affair. I simply nodded for everything unconcernedly, without even letting them know that I was an absolute non-entity in the family.

"Why only in family, even in the entire universe!", my son remarked derisively.

However, I did not react to my son's derisive remark.

In fact, I took those instructions given by the family of the bridegroom as some casual remarks, and did not realise their gravity and import, and the ramifications it would have in the eventuality of their not being fulfilled. I did not have wherewithal to meet those demands, so I had to have a loss of face, not only before my colleagues at school, but also, before the entire marriage party. I was declared a damned fool by my new and old relatives! And a coloured jackal by my colleagues at school!

After the marriage party when I reached my school, the clout I enjoyed earlier was conspicuously absent. They started taking me as a fluke and a fraud, a person with no substance, rather, a hypocrite.

"Whenever someone pretends to be more than what his real worth is, eventually falls even lower in the eyes of fellows than he actually would have fallen." My son sermonised, "Your tale is just on the lines I was surmising it to be; you have always been like that. You cannot think or act anything sensibly."

XXX

29. Contribution Of Utensils

Enter Mother

In the marriage of my sister-in-law, my husband had made no monetary contribution. He was employed as an *ad hoc* teacher at a far off place for a paltry sum which was just enough for his individual's sustenance. When he was not making any contribution despite feigning to be in employ at a far off place, how could he hope to command any respect in the family. First proof of his foolishness was the fact that for a paltry sum of Rs. Two hundred per month he was staying at such a far off place, with his relatives, whilst he could have earned much more than that by working in his agricultural holdings at his village.

During his sister's marriage, again as ever, he resorted to the same recourse – his wife's possessions. Whatever utensils had been gifted by my parents during my marriage, he decided to gift all of them in the marriage of his sister. When the utensils were being taken away from our dwelling to the place of marriage, the altar, my innocent teenager son enquired, "Why are they giving away our wares?"

I assured him that this was the practice, that these utensils had been gifted so many times over the years, during the entire history of those utensils.

I remembered incidentally that this indolent husband of mine had sold off my gold jewellery and the golden bangles of this innocent baby already, and to no avail, simply a wastage; what has he availed, or what is he after all, simply a brat, a bully, a mad man! He could not complete his B. Ed. even, for which purpose he had usurped as well as frittered away my jewellery and the emotive bangles of my baby son! Now he cannot think anything other than frittering away whatever little possessions we have in the form of these utensils.

Thus were gone the utensils of the household!

And as a recompense for the expenses of my sister-in-law's marriage which were incurred all by my husband's elder brother, it was agreed that my husband would not take anything from the produce of the agriculture for unknown number of years.

And this was under this arrangement that in our house for years together we did not receive any harvest even during the harvesting season whereas in other households of the peasants, we saw that the cartloads of grains and cereals came. This scenario of deprivation in respect of agricultural produce despite claiming themselves to be the agriculturists, somewhere engendered a feeling of depression and inferiority complex in my mind, and also, in the minds of my son and other issues. They could not feel themselves belonging to anything there because nothing out of this set up ever was seen coming to their house.

My husband was totally depending on his 'ad hoc' job in school as if that was 'permanent'. As if 'ad hoc' meant 'permanent'! The same was true of his life! He felt as if his life was permanent! And a soul who thinks the phenomena in this Creation as permanent has a very erroneous view, and it is observed that his or her behaviour towards fellow beings and creatures becomes very cruel and callous. One who is in constant know of the fact that everything, every phenomenon and every moment in this Creation is ephemeral turns out to be a suave and polite soul.

Having thus had frittered

away my wares in the marriage of my sister-in-law, I came back to my parents' home with my son and little daughters. During this single year, I had thus become a perfect destitute: having been devoid of a shelter already, now I had become devoid of my utensils. However now I feel in hindsight that it was a precursor to our wretched condition in near future when we did not get even cereals to eat, clothing to wear and hut to seek shelter under; what use were then the utensils for us, as if? God had, therefore, snatched away our roof and now the utensils, the jewellery having already been frittered away.

On what hope I was living I do not know.

Sometimes methinks: what sort of a man my father-in-law was who could enjoy intercourses with his wife and beget issues in the process, but was totally indifferent to his own duties towards those begotten in the name of his own issues! He was least bothered about the marriage of his issues, too, as if that was for the issues themselves to sort out amongst themselves!

Likewise, methinks quite often: what sort of a man I had as my husband who was not at all a fit person to be called a husband in the sense that he could not meet even a single condition for claiming himself to be a husband; and what sort of an 'educated' brat he was that he was unable to afford even a menial job for himself in return, rather, he did squander away whatever little or more he was given in inheritance by his ancestors, and also, whatever little or more he was given in dowry by his in-laws! The turned over leaflets of my life bare this naked truth unabashedly!

XXX

30. Aalhaa-Oodal & Vulgarity Of Urchins

Enter Protagonist

There were only very few dwelling units in our *Naanee*'s village. On one end there were the homesteads of the *Braahmans* who were very suave and gentle by demeanour, and were somewhat poor, too, given their small unviable landholdings and resources. Then there were two influential dwelling units of our *Naanaajee* and elder *Naanaajee*. On the other end of the hamlet there were the dwelling units of two other persons, supposedly, of the same caste as ours but considered to be of 'lowly' demeanour, going by their living standards.

Not only the youngsters, but also, the elders of these dwelling units on the fag end of the village were conspicuously uncivil and 'uncultured'. In every sense! Even in the sense of conduct, not to speak of education and literacy! They seemed to be alike the aborigines, however, claiming themselves to be of 'upper' caste; wisely enough. I, however, have no grudge against anybody claiming oneself to be of 'upper' caste. I, rather, grumble only when someone proclaims oneself to be of 'lower' caste: why should one demean oneself, of one's own volition?

Those two dwelling units had multitudes of children and all of them were invariably bad behaved, vulgar and unpolished; even so, their elders were. They were seen untidy, and clad savagely, too. Yet because one of them studied in the same class as I was studying in, and in the same school, we oftentimes went together treading the narrow footpaths on the banquettes of the fields. This particular boy was respectful towards me, though; maybe due to my stature as a brilliant boy of the school. He was hefty bodied nonetheless, and I could not challenge him physically; therefore, I took care not to squabble with him, even though I had the invincible support of my maternal household.

These two dwelling units were very fond of reciting *Aalhaa,* the folk epic of valour of medieval era. It depicted the valour of two warlords of tribesmen of *Bundelkhand, Aalhaad Raav* and *Ulhaas Raav*, colloquially and fondly called as *Aalhaa* and *Oodal.*

Aalhaa Oodal bade ladaiyaa

Jinkee maar sahee naa jaay!
(*Aalhaa* and *Oodal* were great warriors; their assault was impossible to resist!)

This used to be the refrain of the valiant ballads of this epic. Not only in their household, at other spots as well, this epic was very popular in that area. My assessment is that the inmates of those two bizarre dwelling units would have been from the tribe of *Aalhaa* and *Oodal* only, the tribesmen themselves; for their demeanour, conduct, culture *et al* matched more with those rustic tribesmen, not with our civilized maternal family.

My *Naanaajee* had an attitude of aversion towards these rascals and rustic creatures, from top to bottom. I could never fathom the underlying cause behind that attitude of my *Naanaajee* towards them, even as, I never saw my *Naanaajee* converse with them. Of course, all other members of our family including our *Maamaajee* used to interact with them normally; but never our *Naanaajee.*

Anyone could hear the refrains of *Aalhaa* emanating from their dwellings, to one's amusement.

Anyway, all through the year the unassuming boy did not show any signs of rancour and envy towards me; nonetheless, when the final exams were over and the result was out, and I was declared first, not only in school, but also, in the entire

Exam Centre, and when I was thrilled to receive the happy news from the mouth of my teacher, this boy commented with a sense of envy and pique, "I am also first, in the whole of Centre!"

This derisive comment coming as it did from the lips of a mediocre boy pricked the balloon of my ego and arrogance, to contemplate that even if one did not secure the first position, one could very easily as well as safely declare oneself to be the first; who was going to verify the veracity of the claim! So far as verification was concerned, my claim was not being verified, too. In this way, I realised the futility of standing first in the school, or topping the Centre etc. It was all fake and fluke and inconsequential. All these phenomena: of prestige, position and achievements! Everybody considers oneself most intelligent, and nobody gets happy at the news of somebody else's standing first; everybody envies everybody. The human world is like that only. I realised this truth for the first time.

On the issue of having a tussle with this boy, my *Maamaajee* tried to prop me up quite often encouraging me with the words that I should pick that loafer up and throw him down on the ground in the style of *Bheem,* the mythological hero of *Mahaabhaarat.* However, I could never gather that much courage: to throw him down on the ground and thrash him.

Whether it was the fallout of recitation of *Aalhaa,* the poetry of valour and strife, I can't say, but it was felt that the offspring being brought up in those households had developed the traits of belligerence and a fighting spirit in their genes. Alike the medieval age wayfarers, looters and *pindaarees,* to be precise, they also had no qualms about resorting to anti-social activities. Their christening being after the appellations of great men and gods, e.g.; *Krishna (Kishunaa), Bhagwaan (Bhagwaanaa), Vasudev, et al,* notwithstanding, they were indulged in all sorts of nefarious activities including dacoities. At least one of their offspring, named *Bhagwaanaa* when he came up of age took to forming part of a local dacoity gang which was formed by some like-minded louts of the area. This fact was known to the inhabitants of the area well, but nobody dared report the same to police or authorities. We observed that earlier when those louts were not actively involved in real dacoities, their countenance and demeanour looked amiable at least to some extent, but now, after they were engrossed in the unethical act of dacoities, their countenances and demeanours had assumed demoniac forms; their eyes had become scarlet coloured thereafter, their tones had become brusque and abrasive.

People including us fellow kids wondered how those wayward youths could expect to live a peaceful and worthwhile life getting indulged in such heinous crimes.

Later on, this boy, *Bhagwaanaa* fell in the hands of police; and I suspect someone might have informed the police. His parents and family members entreated my *naanaajee* for getting him bail by standing a guarantor for him. My *Naanaajee* was reluctant to oblige at first, but when some close relatives in the village insisted, he relented, and the dacoit got the bail. Nevertheless, a few years later his sins caught up with him and *Bhagwaanaa* was reported to have been killed in an encounter. Our *naanaajee* and we all were so glad! A daemon had been done with! This episode clarified to me that daemons are not something extra-terrestrial or subterranean species, they are developed very much amidst us all, amidst the society only.

XXX

31. K-68, New Wheat Strain & Green Revolution

Enter protagonist

This was the year 1967, the winter season. The season had just set in and we were in the process of changing the sheets on our cots – straw cots were in vogue - from those suitable for summer to those suitable for winter's chill, the cold. I used to sleep with my *Naanaajee* in the big *Chaupaal* – male drawing room – which was located at the front portion of the female portion of the residence. When it came to providing me with a woollen or a thick cotton sheet, I refused to take it contending that it was not that cold for me, and that I enjoyed sleeping covered under a thin summer-worthy sheet. As if to show my valour! My virility! As if they were going to reward me for this foolhardiness! But I was merely a lad, an adolescent chap, totally unmindful of the vagaries as well as realities of mother Nature.

Nonetheless, this show of strength and expression of the same before my *Naanaajee* – whom I, of course, called *Baabaa* – was a topic of chit-chat among the village folks and in the small area. And this gossip about my 'greatness' based on the sham show of machismo, merely on the basis of not accepting a woollen sheet, was a source of conceit for me. I enjoyed it; however, ultimately to give in when it started to become colder, and my caring mother and particularly my *Naanee,* who were wiser than I was, forcefully provided me with a quilt, subconsciously to my relief. Sometimes false show of 'greatness' becomes *galey kee haddee* (a bone as if stuck in the flesh of throat)!

In that soothing *Chaupaal,* whose walls were adorned with

dozens of calendars and pictures, I and my *Naanaajee* slept the yearlong in complete comfort. In that *Chaupaal,* my *Naanaajee* used to dictate letters – post cards – off and on addressed to his eldest grandson, the son of our elder *Maamaajee,* in whose marriage party, incidentally, we had gone by bullock-cart. He was employed at *Aagaraa* with the IRCTC. A peculiarity of these letters that invariably struck or moved me was that *Naanaajee* used to dictate them in a very formal style: he instructed me to write address and salutations 'formally' first of all before starting his dictation. Sometimes our *Maamaajee* also used to come to the *chaupaal* when we would be writing the letter, and he used to add his views to be conveyed to his only son. His son and my *Maamaajee* were seldom seen conversing with each other personally; they rather behaved like born adversaries, given my *Maamaajee*'s irascible and ever irrational demeanour; not everybody could stand my *Maamaajee*'s harsh behaviour.

One thing that I did not like while writing those postcards dictated by *Naanaajee* was that *Naanaajee* asked me to write to his grandson that the crops that year were not good and that the produce was scanty. In fact, in my heart somewhere, I harboured the notion that my maternal family were quite wealthy and had large landholdings, and therefore had no reason that their harvest should not be quite profuse, by any standards. *Naanaajee* might be right in his conviction and in terms of bars set by him for his harvest, but I somehow felt that he was downplaying the agricultural performance so as to impress his grandson to contribute something monetarily to the family fold, which he never did, in my knowledge. The service class people, though seemingly earning on behalf of the entire family folks, do actually confine their earnings to themselves, and if at all, to their immediate family only.

The wider family members should, therefore, not hope too much from those who are employed somewhere that they would contribute anything to the common family coffers.

In this *Chaupaal* only, we saw the Green Revolution ushered in to India. New strains of wheat were being developed, being put to practical use in the agricultural fields; resultantly, the crops were exceptionally rich that year. One such novel strain of wheat developed or invented that year was *K-68,* (pronounced *'kay adashath'*), possibly signifying the year 1968, when the wheat would be harvested. Thus far in the past, the crops were not that rich, those were yielding only modicum produce. The new strains of cereals did change the scenario significantly; that was sort of a paradigm shift in the agricultural field. The farmers were getting induced towards use of chemical fertilisers for boosting their produce. Earlier, they used only the organic manure – the cattle and human waste – in their fields, and were content with the modicum yields only whatever could be produced. The chemical fertiliser was not easily available everywhere; people used various mechanisms to procure a sack of fertiliser, even going to the extent of paying premium to the black marketeers. That was yet another contribution, another 'feather' in the cap of achievements, of the ruling regime post-Independence! I can still recollect, in that year, on the day of *Badaa Din* – the Christmas – my *Naanaa* had asked me to accompany him to the nearby Railway station. On my asking what the purpose of going their was, or who was coming by train, my *Naanaajee* didn't disclose anything to me. On the way and on reaching the railway station, I remained under spell of that mystery. Finally, when the passenger train from the nearby town where my younger *Maamaajee* served did arrive I could come to know that it was my younger *Maamaajee* who had come and had brought a sackful of chemical fertiliser, the Urea, which was such a

buzzword those days, and was considered to be a sort of magical concoction, by using which, the agricultural yield could be enhanced multiple times. Who would not be lured! We – I and my *Naanaajee* – carried that sackful of load on our heads by dividing it in two unequal parts from station to the village. Why I recollect this trifling episode I don't know; maybe due to the primacy of ephemerality of everything including memorable times and pleasurable incidents!

During the same year in the season of *Dashaharaa* and *Diwaalee,* my *Naanaa* took me along on a long journey to the nearby town, almost 25 kms away, all on foot. I was ten at that time, and he an adult of 70 or so. I travelled that distance without any grudge, rather happily. My *Baabaa* was highly impressed by my vigour and virility, and praised me in the village after returning. On the long way, however, along the water brook, we had a rare opportunity to watch the green fields as a testimony to the success of Green Revolution. And the triumph of biotech science, in a sense!

XXX

Enter Naanaajee

One day, as usual, I decided to visit the nearby town, the purpose being to purchase the monthly provisions required for running and upkeep of the household. I did this sortie once in a month, and I took the route to the town via *Jaabil* and *Dushehraa*. Both the villages were pretty afar from our hamlet, almost 4 or 5 kms apart. The intention to go this way was so as to take a conveyance, either a bus if swiftly available, or one of the *tongaas* that plied quite frequently, and were easy to handle, too, for they provided lot of leeway to the passengers in the manner of getting onto and getting down.

I took my daughter's son – the protagonist – along with me on this journey; it proved to be a good support for me to carry the bags of provisions. Earlier on, during one such journey, instead of taking recourse to *tongaa* or a bus, going to *Dushehraa* first, we had undertaken the journey on foot, both to and from the town.

In our *tongaa* this time, there were several passengers, some ladies, some gents. They were carrying their luggage, too, in the *tongaa*, for in the countryside, the cereals and agricultural produce are the only means of exchange, the cash being scarce. One of our co-passengers was carrying a sackful of some agricultural produce for selling in the town, possibly in turn to purchase the monthly provisions. In post-British India, somehow, there had been imposed so many types of

taxes, octrois etc. that one could not carry even one's produce from one's village to the town without paying the octroi at the Octroi post.

Before the town, at about a km ahead, there was an octroi post: a ramshackle brickwork as the octroi office, and one or two cartoon type persons occupying the wooden chairs. The persons carrying their produce were supposed to approach them for paying the octroi. However, at the post, the person who was carrying the luggage in the *tongaa,* seeing my grandson as a youth, asked him to go pay the octroi. With slight hesitation and after my nod, my grandson obliged the adult and reached the cartoons. They enquired certain things, to which, the concerned person – the owner -- only replied to them. They wrote a handwritten receipt and returned some change to the protagonist. He picked the both, and handed the same to the gentleman, and boarded the *tongaa*. The *tongaa* started moving.

Hardly had the *tongaa* moved half a furlong, that the gentleman whom my boy had assisted squeaked, 'How much change you have brought?'

'Whatever they returned I gave you!', the boy replied, surprised at the sudden change of tone of the scoundrel.

'But the receipt is for such and such amount; the change should have been that much!'

'But he returned me only that much!', the boy was losing patience thinking that he had done him a favour whereas he was none to him; and he was now repaying the boy in those terms, accusing the latter of embezzlement.

'You should have checked both the receipt and the exchange!' the man commented and added derisively, 'This is the result of education gained on the strength of money earned through *soodkhoree* (usury)!....'

At this remark of his, I took exception and rejoindered, however politely, that the money being spent on the education of the boy was hard earned money of a peasant, not of a usurer. I also added that the boy was a very brilliant student of his school. At this, the gentleman whom I had by now taken to be a scoundrel and ungrateful person kept quiet, simply saying that he was not commenting particularly about me, but that the boy should have checked the change before leaving the counter.

I clarified that it was due to the inexperience of the young boy about such things: corruption prevalent in the post-British regime. About the rampant corruption of Govt officials post-British India!

This seemingly trifling incident hurt my heart badly and made an indelible impression on my heart, and also, on the heart of the boy. Throughout the day in town I kept on ruminating about this humiliation at the hands of a scoundrel, a stranger whom the boy had assisted, which he should not have done. He should not have been helped. No stranger should ever be helped in such cases, particularly, involving Govt. offices and officers.

When we returned home, I narrated this episode to the family members, for I was still feeling the hurt, especially, about the imputation that the money earned by us was the money earned through *sood* (interest). The boy commented about this that *soodkhoree* as a means of earning was considered to be abominable in those days. I nodded in acceptance.

However, one of my grandsons, *Raajendra* clarified that at such posts as octroi etc. it was a norm to cheat the taxpayers, for they issue receipt on the basis of whatever the owner declares; therefore, they deduct a cut as their personal income apart from the octroi from the money given by the public. This clarification gave me and the boy ample amount of solace. Nonetheless, it filled me with an angst thinking as to what sort of Independent India these disciples of *Gaandhee* had created: all scoundrels, thugs and thieves! What impression the child had taken I don't know.

XXX

Table of Contents

33. Panchaayat *Elections and Social Fabric Getting Torn apart*

Enter Protagonist

The days of green revolution were bringing smile on the faces of peasants including my maternal relatives with whom we were sheltered. The olden ways of cultivation and agriculture were seeing a definite change. There was change in the thinking of new generation. The old ways and old thinking could no more do, people had come to realise.

Nevertheless, nothing such sort of revolution in the thinking of my paternal set-up was visible; they were still under the hangover of their past glories, on the ruins of which only the new setup of Governance and administration had been raised.

Every five years, they were conducting elections for electing various types of representatives to run the system of the country, and *Panchaayat* elections were the quintessence of that neo procedure of Governance. *Panchaayats* were supposed to be the fulcrum upon which the mansion of the new genie, the 'Democracy', was to be based. Earlier, however, there was no such provision, rather only the writ of the landlord, the *zameendaar*, ran. Now the entire scenario was supposed to have changed.

Nonetheless, during the elections that were taking place that year – 1967 – I observed that the people, particularly, our relatives who commuted from the towns and cities for their jobs daily, used to bring home the saddening news of rifts rising by the day in the society owing explicitly to the *Panchaayat* elections. They brought the news one day that a youth had been murdered in broad day light by his opponents who were against his contesting for the post of village head – the *Pradhaan*. Another commuter brought the saddening news the other day that two brothers had shot each other's families for they were running for election to the *Panchaayat* posts. Also, on yet another day that a corpse had been recovered from the wayside wettles and was recognised as the body of a candidate for *Panchaayat* elections. Some of these news were based on the grapevine, some conveyed as hearsay, and most of this stuff came by way of news reports. A peculiarity of the phenomenon was that one or two depressing news arrived daily in that small hamlet.

The settlement being quite small and closely knit together, it was but natural that all the elders would huddle together in the evenings at the *chaupaal* of the most prominent person – and that prominent person was our maternal grandfather – and would discuss minute details and ramifications of the incidents. Also, they tried to find the way out of such maladies that were stalking the society, even as, the remedies suggested would be too far-fetched and at times mirthful, too.

I being a child wondered and still do that the human society is not that safe and secure as it seems to be. Its structure is quite fragile in fact. Its stability depends on the clout of the dominant person of society. If there is no single dominant person in society whom everybody regards as one's saviour, or the ruler, it is quite possible that the society would be destroyed and might go wayward and anarchic.

I also wondered and still do that the election process, though envisaged for the good of the society, is necessarily proving to be a fissiparous element for it. The social fabric is getting torn apart in the process, rather. Instead of being an opportunity for serving the society, the election victories have assumed the status of winning the chance for looting the society nonchalantly and unaccountably. Definitely, something wrong has taken place in the name of election phenomenon. It has engendered so many fissiparous tendencies in the minds of scoundrels to divide the society on the lines of caste, creed, sub-castes, religion, sect *et al.* The same calm and serene villages which resembled Elysium in our imagination were rife with heart-wrenching incidents merely because

of this new system called elections and *Panchaayats.*

XXX

34. Twig Of Neem (Margosa) & Death Of A Child

Enter Protagonist

Childish conceit or arrogance may wreak havoc with its possessor's prestige and image irreparably. I being a declared gifted prodigy of the school and family, and a hope for my father's indolent wretched family, I could never think that anything could be beyond my grasp or there could be anything which I could not do.

One such incident took place during this year only. Actually, my elder *Naanaa*'s elder son was a simpleton, rather a buffoon. Not only the grown-ups, but also, the children of all ages made fun of him as if he were a child of their own age only. They played pranks on him care-freely without any regard to his sensibilities, and he did not have any sensibilities, too, it seemed by his demeanour; he rather enjoyed all such buffoonery. Children even commented obscenely about him, and even obscene content was involved in their merriment.

When husband was of that sort – albeit to the dislike of his own father, my elder *Naanaajee* – his wife had also become a butt of joke at the hands of urchins of the tiny sized village. She was not of deranged or loose mind, though; she was a serene type of lady, but did not mind people cutting jokes on her, too. I was one of the tormentors of the husband and wife, both, being only a teenager; not even a teenager yet, in fact.

Incidentally, during the season of watermelons, in their house one summer day, watermelons were bought and their grandson who was a very handsome cherub chap consumed excessively followed by intake of water. It is a conventional wisdom that drinking of water over the intake of watermelon results in fatality, for it is supposed to choke the food pipe, or the respiratory duct.

The child fell ill and all sorts of treatments and medications were administered, all manner of places he was taken to, but providentially to no avail. The condition only kept on deteriorating day by day.

In this backdrop, not realising the gravity of the situation or the imminent tragedy, I made a blunder: it so happened that the simpleton and serene wife of that simpleton husband emerged from her house. She was the grandmother of the fatally sick lad. She approached me at the *Chaupaal* of *Naanaajee* where I was playing all alone floating in the glory of my

wisdom as well as false arrogance. The sober lady requested me to pluck a twig from the *Neem* tree, to which, however, I could not relate myself as to the cause thereof. She, in fact, wanted that twig for doing some *Jhaad-Foonk* (quack treatment) for his fatally ill grandson, but I could not realise the gravity; how could I, I was not briefed by anybody in this behalf. Nor did I know that death could come so abruptly to anybody! The extremely and abnormally morose face of the lady also failed to arouse any sense of sanity in my mind. I stuck to my childish guns and refused to pluck a twig from our *Neem* tree. Somewhere in my subconscious mind I had an idea to have fun with the simpleton lady as we usually used to do. She repeated her entreaties, going even to the extremes of politeness, but in my foolishness I could not come to senses. Ultimately the sober lady contorted her face and commented extremely contemptuously against me which I could not comprehend, but I was surprisingly shocked to see that queer behaviour towards me; she was not usually like that. Nonetheless, she was face to face with the prospect of death of her dearest kin at that juncture!

She went back and then came another lady, her mother-in-law, the wife of our elder *Naanaajee*. She also pleaded with me in vain and went back, too. A simple twig! And I kept on commenting, 'Why should we disfigure our *Neem* tree by plucking the twigs from it?' Perfectly childish! Feeling in my heart that I was doing some inexorable misdeed, *akushal karm,* notwithstanding.

Hardly had the old lady gone back that there started coming the loud wails from their house. I was shocked indeed. I had not foreseen that much; I was simply having fun. There was death in toe, I didn't know! Had I known in advance I would not have behaved that insanely and callously.

I was shocked. However, I tried to draw solace in the idea that the adult lady and the old lady would forget everything in the melee of wailing and death that appeared on the scene just after my sinful misdemeanour. Since the death was heart-rending, the youth being hardly seven or eight years old, there was abnormal spell of sorrow on the entire village, and also, in the relationships.

Nevertheless, the misdeed I had done just as a precursor to death, came to light immediately, without any time-gap. The ladies wailed during their lamentations that had I given a twig of *Neem* to them their grandson would have survived the fatal illness. Accusing an innocent child in front of the gathering like this was horrible for my maternal family. My mother did feel embarrassed but did not say anything to me; she knew that I was a child and casting aspersions on an innocent child of hardly ten was a perfect nonsense. But the pain and sorrow of death makes the mind to resort to any sort of accusations wherever one finds solace. If they derived some solace in this accusation, there was no harm!

However, my *Naanee,* my *Naanaajee* and my *Maamaajee,* took exception to this childish accusation on the part of the grandees of the deceased boy, and they rebuked me in mock derision asking me why I had not given the twigs to the ladies. I could discern the mockery of their reprimand, however, and did not mind too much.

I might not have minded my misdeed but the two ladies did, and their family members including the mother of the untimely deceased boy did too; they never ever thereafter talked to me amicably, rather, whenever they faced me, the shapes of their countenance exhibited utter dislike for me, and a sense of revengefulness. For I was the instrument of the death that took away their most precious gem from the family!

They never spoke to me thereafter, whereas earlier they always behaved very sweetly as well as affably with me. Self-interest is the most prominent factor in the inter-personal behaviours in the living world, I realised. Life has primacy when it comes to life and death! And that ought to be honoured!

This childish *faux pas* on my part I have never been able to forget. Incidentally, both the ladies died soon thereafter – within a year or so -- possibly not standing the strain of untimely death of their grandson and great grandson, respectively. His mother, of course, was quite young; she had to bear this burden of calamity throughout her life; therefore, she continued to live. I did too! But with the constant haunting by the memory of this painful incident, on which I had no command possibly but, of which, I was considered a culprit.

XXX

35. Kraanti Deedee *And My Mother*

Enter Mother

Libido is such a queer phenomenon which does not bother about other considerations or norms framed by human society; framed for its normal conduct. My father had begotten five surviving issues: an elder son followed by two daughters, then a son and a daughter. I was the last one in this chain. However, unlike at present when the issues are begotten quite swiftly almost immediately after getting married, in those olden days when marriages were solemnised at an early age, the issues were begotten quite patiently and with ample gaps between two issues. This might be the reason that we siblings were amply spaced in ages.

Nonetheless, by the time I was born, my eldest brother had already been married; and married in a well to do family like ours only. I was conceived obviously after my brother had already been married. That's why I exclaim that libido is such a bizarre phenomenon; it does not mind any manner of abashment. Why I am surmising that I was conceived after my brother already had his young wife in our household, for after my birth, it was not long that my niece – the daughter of my brother was born, too. *Kraantee! Kraantee* was the name given her by the *Panditjee*. And I feel, it would have been inspired by the revolution taking place in the country in the guise of national movement in those days. And me? I was named *Phool,* the flower; and in light vein, a fool, if it's taken in English! I might have been quite pretty at birth, that's why *'Phool'*, a flower!

There was thus not much of a difference in our ages – the ages of *Phool* and *Kraantee*. Nonetheless, this short difference in the ages of the daughters of a father and a son, in my view, possibly had been the cause of bad blood having developed between my father and my brother, for in my memory, I had never seen them speaking normally with each other. Whenever they interacted, they interacted like strangers, like born adversaries.

When we grew up, being almost of the same ages, we – *Kraantee* and I – were antagonists mutually, as was natural between two kids of almost the same age. We were sort of competitors, envious of each other. That's a normal human tendency.

I was the daughter of the father and the mother of even the father of *Kraantee*; she would be at the receiving end always by those yardsticks. Otherwise also, I was a puffed up girl child, always insolent, ever throwing my weight around on the basis of my being the daughter of my father *'Baaboo Singh'*. And I pronounced this sentence – sort of warning - quite often whenever I needed to threaten somebody. Such children free of worries of existence as they are, they become frank and develop a hilarious sense of humour, too. I was frank and very jolly natured and was also endowed with an exceptional sense of humour.

Kraantee was however a sober and good tempered girl, even so, her mother – my *Bhaabhee*, the sister-in-law -- was good natured, civilized and an educated lady; she used to read *Bhagwad Geetaa* daily, for reportedly her deceased father

had instructed her to that effect. Not only the wife, even my brother – her husband – used to read *Geetaa* quite often; he had a copy of *Bhagwad Geetaa* kept in his room that was situated at a corner of the sprawling house towards the wilderness or the thoroughfare, so to say. He was sort of a watchman, a sentinel, for the household, and the guard for the female folks, female residences. How fragile is the social set up! Every night we go to sleep absolutely at the mercy of anti-social elements! Unless there is proper arrangement of safety and security of our household, or in broader sense, unless there is proper system to maintain law and order in the society, the area or the country, for that matter, there can be no mental peace, nor any well-being.

Though my brother did not go to school beyond basic classes, all his issues – in all four – were endowed with regal personalities, and were sharp brained and looked naturally cultured.

Coming back to *Kraantee,* my born source of envy, she had been to school and I could not due to circumstances I have already narrated earlier in this tale. *Kraantee* thus had an advantage or edge over me. Nonetheless, in those days of British India, being illiterate or uneducated was no demerit by any standards, especially, for girls; rather, it was considered to be an added feather in the cap for girls! Still I always felt inferior to my niece when it came to matters intellectual.

How my parents handled the matters involving their own dearest daughter and their granddaughter, I can't say, but my elder brother treated both of us equally harshly and without any remorse; he was a tyrant incarnate without doubt. Who had instructed him to be harsh towards one and all, particularly, towards young kids, only God knows who was his creator!

We grew up struggling and squabbling and came of age, being the source of worry for our respective parents. But given the sound financial condition of the family, courtesy of large land holdings, finding worthy bridegrooms for us was no brainer for the family elders. Still marrying female folks was a herculean task in those days. Dowry by then had not been declared illegal, or was not considered a matter of shame in the society at large!

Eventually, the boys were found out for us. Paradoxically, for me, the illiterate one, a lad who was outwardly proclaimed as literate and supposedly endowed with so many virtues. And on top of that, from a 'feudal' family!

Kraantee, on the other hand, was married too in almost equally wealthy family of landlords and feudal lords, but paradoxically not to such a lad who had very good education and enviable prospects.

At that juncture, it seemed as though I was at a vantage point. But who can read the cards of Providence! That's why I used the term 'paradox'!

It turned out otherwise, just the opposite: my husband turned out to be a non-entity, a deranged personality who squandered everything, mind everything whatever there was in possession of the family, whereas *Kraantee* was living with her husband at the latter's place of posting in *Jhaansee* quite comfortably. I was all along living at my parents' house despite being married, my husband was serving as an *ad hoc* teacher in some private school at some remote village! The fact of the matter is that he was an *ad hoc* teacher for merely half a dozen years and in as many schools, from where he was eased out within a year or two necessarily. For the most part of his life, he was merely a petty tutor who taught English grammar and translation to village children.

During this one year of our exile also, *Kraantee* happened to visit the village, and I fondly wished I were in her place instead of mine. My parents also felt the same sense of loss at seeing their own favourite daughter, whom they loved so much, being in an inverted vortex of fate!

There used to be an undercurrent of envy, jealousy or tussle in the matters concerning *Kraantee* and me, which even my parents and the parents of *Kraantee* felt palpably. This concerned not only the presents or parting gifts given, but also, the fates of us two. But who could help all this?

It was *Kraantee* only who had suggested my elder son's – the protagonist's – name, she being an intellectual lady. My son relished his name so much and felt obliged to *Kraantee* for having given him such a beautiful name when he came to know of the fact that this was *Kraantee* who had given him his name. People often say: 'what is in a name?' But there is a lot in a name only!

Nonetheless, my experience suggests that a good sounding and well-meaning name matters a lot in life and in job, in career and also in later life. Maybe that is why the progenies of well off families prefer civilized and soothing names, whereas the poor folks contend with absurd names, they are not allowed to have good sounding names for their kids; and it all seems to have been done by design: to keep the wretched ones as wretched ones only, in perpetuity! People contend 'what is in a name?'; I say there's a lot in name, and also, in fame!

XXX

36. Raamaayan, Romance And Calamity

Enter Protagonist

Another salutary impression on my impressionable life during that year of exile in my maternal households was the presence of my maternal cousins. Besides those two school going cousins of almost my age, there were two more cousins of somewhat elder age: one, the middle daughter of my elder *maamaajee,* and the other one, the eldest daughter of my younger *maamaajee.* They were both unmarried by that time and were, of course, approaching marriageable ages. And were, therefore, supposed to be presentable biological commodities! Social set up being such that the marital connections could be normally feasible only within a constricted sphere – the sphere of the same caste - the parents and grandparents of such young lasses were constantly on the lookout for prospective lads who could be harnessed as their matching bridegrooms.

During that one year, I also observed that my younger *maamaajee* had been transferred from the normal city where he usually remained throughout his service career to a town relatively tiny and closer by. He used to commute almost daily from there to his village. The set-up of society at my maternal household being such that even girls were supposed to work in the agricultural fields and perform all sorts of tasks involving strenuous physical labour, these two elder cousins of mine were subjected to all sorts of hard labour. They were of good conduct and demeanours, of course, no doubt!

For our *Naanaa's* house was quite large and spacious, during the summer and salubrious seasons, we slept under the sky, beneath the stars, in the sprawling courtyard of the big house. There, to beat the time, our elder cousin – the daughter of elder *Maamaajee* – decided to narrate the story of *Raamaayan* to us children. The story of *Raam* and *Raamaayan* was as yet unknown to us, of course! Therefore, when our benevolent and kind sister – cousin – ventured to tell that moralising tale to us, we picked up interest in the storyline; we rather would wait for the fall of dusk so that we could listen to the interesting and intriguing story daily. Moreover, the style of our cousin while narrating the story was very engrossing: she kept on expounding the nuances of the tale for us children. She also removed our doubts and suspicions wherever we found the storyline unreasonable or preposterous. She sometimes clarified the causative factors, and also, the psychological phenomena working at the back of some developments in the story.

We were relishing the supposedly unending tale: we thought that the tale of *Raam* and *Raamaayan* would be unending. Alike the tale of life! Life itself in the entire Creation, not the individual's life, which is ephemeral!

However, that was not to be! Once it so happened that in the process of threshing the corn from the corncobs by beating the piles of corn by thick wooden sticks, the fingers of my cousins got wounded; and since this was merely a village, a hamlet, rather, there were no facilities of medication or medical consultation, or not even the Dettol to soak the bruises with, the hurts did aggravate soon enough due to neglect, and in turn developed septic. The pain became excruciating. My cousins used to cry and sigh in unbearable agony at night, and we kids were helpless. We could not help in any manner except feeling sorry and sad for both of them whole-heartedly; that we did. In the process, the story of our *Raamaayan* was set aside, and for good. It could not be revived even later on, under the ever changing scenarios, seasons and circumstances of the rustic life.

When the septic calamity became intolerable for not only the girls, but also, for the elders of the family, my younger *maamaajee* took both of them to the town where he had been serving, and had been transferred that year. The septic could be cured ultimately; at least that much progress had been made in the medical arena in India post-Independence!

However, in that town, where my *maamaajee* had rented a room for stay, there also lived one or two lads of the same caste we belonged to. The same age almost as my cousins were! It was a God-sent opportunity as though! Nothing bashful about it! After all, young girls must needs to be found some boys for getting them married to. These boys hailed, incidentally, from our paternal village, and were known to our paternal family. However prospective, wealthy, hale and hearty they might be, but our paternal feudal set up did not consider them worthy of wedding to these two girls of a pedigreed family. There used to be so much enthusiasm those days in our maternal household centred around those prospective and seductive lads! Our cousins too appeared to be pretty impressed and romanticised by those prospective husbands!

The septic did get cured, the young girls did return to their village, however, the euphoria that was generated due to proximity of young lads and lasses also subsided, chiefly due to the sanctimonious hypocrisy of the families of our paternal village. They themselves being worthless fellows could not stand any progressive family, particularly, in their village, and in their immediate proximity. That is typical of feudal systems!

XXX

37. Hardly A Bullock-Cart Driver

Enter Protagonist

However brilliant you might be by grace of God or Providence, that's no guarantee for your prestigious future. I might have been basking in the glory of my brilliance at the matters scholarly; in the eyes of society around, I now feel in hindsight, I was merely a wretch, the son of a lovely as well as influential lass who had a husband who had, incidentally, no wherewithal to arrange food, clothing and shelter for his family, and consequently, his family was constrained to stay at his in-law's. How much respect such a family or its individual members could command amongst the social set-up where they happened to dwell? None at all, in absolute terms, however, pretentious they might look, despite the fact that the refugees comprised none other than the dearest as well as youngest daughter of the who's who of the hamlet and her two issues.

Nonetheless, I the child had no such inkling, nor was I bothered in the least in this behalf; I had virtually taken this abode of my maternal relatives as my own.

Incidentally, it was very late in life – rather when I had completed the High School exam – that it dawned upon me palpably that I was not a rightful owner of that carefree shelter.

The reason was that they never let us realise this pinching as well as mind-boggling reality as such! Such congenial was their demeanour!

Still, one day, my *naanaajee* asked me to accompany him to *Bhoodaa*, the village I had been to so many times and had associated with it so many memories sweet and sour including the episode of saw and my alleged indolence. The causative factor behind my frequenting that village so quite often was that there lived in that village the carpenter-cum-blacksmith. He was sort of a lynch-pin for all the implements agrarian for the whole of rural area. Whatever little snag did appear, he was the person to be called and summoned. No, he was not the permanent inhabitant of that hamlet; rather, he hailed from some other village and lived there for eking out his livelihood somehow temporarily. Maybe someone, or the owner of the land where he had a straw-hut raised, had invited him to the village so that he could come handy in agricultural pursuits as regards implements and snags developing therein. He was a gentle and suave guy, docile and responsive; what

else could he be? He was living at the mercy of the rascals and rustics! He was staying there with his young and seductive wife, as all the wives of such wretched labourers invariably are supposed to be. She seemed to be an utterly shy lady; what else could she be? She was living amongst feudal set-up. And amidst lecherous louts!

My *naanaajee* took me along this time in connection with a bullock cart – a small sized vehicle, not a standard sized bullock cart – which had been ordered to be built at the carpenter's village. That day it was to be delivered; my *maamaajee* and I had inspected it being built many a time before that day. It was reported to have been completed, and we were going to take its delivery, to fetch it from *Bhoodaa*. It wasn't a normal day; the weather was not normal, the sky was overcast – abnormally as well as untimely.

At the village, in the compound of a rich farmer, where the cart was being assembled or built, my *naanaajee* had a few old men of his age, and he chatted with them for some time on issues immaterial, mostly on the weather. Merely to fill the time till the cart was made 'ready for go!' People in those days talked together, unlike these days! And they showed ample amount of mutual regard and camaraderie towards one another, unlike these days!

After a while the weather became clear and salubrious, too, and the carpenter declared the cart ready. And we ventured to depart. How? A bullock cart does not run on petroleum fuel! We had taken our bullocks along. The bullocks were yoked to the cart and we set off on journey back to our hamlet, I and my *Naanaa*! After bidding respectful farewell to the landlords of the compound!

First, my *naanaa* took command of the cart and the bulls. He drove them on the *kutcha* path, the dust way. After sometime when the village had been left behind and we were amidst the barren fields on the way, my *naanaa* asked me to take the reins and drive the bullocks. That was shocking to me; I had never driven the bullocks or a bullock cart, nor had I ever imagined in my wildest dreams that I would ever have to be obliged to drive a bullock cart. This small cart was somewhat like a *Tongaa,* an *Ekkaa,* and was got constructed for ferrying the guests to and from the railway station, or even somewhere else. We called it *Rehloo.* In fact, I felt, that so many guests did visit our maternal household every year! And so far, my maternal household did not have a suitable cart, they relied on others for that facility. They, of course, had a big old cart which was used for multiple purposes, including that for

carrying manure and cow dung etc. to the fields, and had been soiled badly in the process, being unfit for the guests.

When my *naanaa* asked me to drive the bullocks and the cart, I did not refuse, thinking that it would be something very easy. I thought that the bullocks would carry the cart of their own, by using their common sense, and that I had simply to sit there and make some insensible noise, like, *tik-tik, aa-haa* as was made by the drivers of bullock carts as observed by me. I took the reins, and *naanaajee* gave me, too, without any thought whatsoever. He had seen me accompanying his grandson – *Surendradaa* – who used to drive the bullock cart quite so often and quite so dexterously. By that impression he might have thought that I would be an exponent, too, of bullock cart driving.

Within no time, I came to the realisation and quite palpably that it was not a joke to control and command the bullocks yoked in a cart; also, that the bulls do not move on their own, they have to be guided and commanded assertively constantly and have to be given the impression that someone is there sitting on their head. Who would hit them if they falter or show signs of recalcitrance! As soon as the seasoned bullocks heard the sweet and innocuous voice of a child, they decided to revolt forthwith. Where is our master? Who is this novice? Who says *tik-tik* when he ought to say *aa-haa*! They went berserk and out of way, too. My *naanaajee* had the shock of his life; I didn't have the guts to control the bulls, nor the simple skill to drive a bullock cart! Very sad! He was not prepared for this eventuality as if! With utter disgust, he exclaimed, "You do not know even how to drive a bullock cart?"

"No, *Baabaa*! I don't know how to drive a bullock cart."

"But you should have learnt; all our boys have this skill, it's strange and depressing that you have not acquired even this simple skill!"

I felt deeply humiliated when he said this.

Naanaajee further added, "What are you learning for last one year in your school?"

I gazed into his seasoned face, totally amazed at this crazy remark of his.

He continued with a melancholy face and sombre voice, "How shall you live your life; how shall you complete your life's journey without even having the skills to drive a bullock cart? It is so essential to know how to drive a bullock cart!"

Naanaajee had already taken command of the bullocks and they were now carrying the cart like very civilized creatures, as if after knowing that someone aged and someone of their ilk was sitting on their head!

'Rascals!' I thought, 'Even these beasts know whom to cooperate with, and whom to revolt against! Pure nepotism! Pure favouritism!....Pure bestialism!'

My maternal grandfather was utterly morose while making all those utterances. He seemed to be absolutely sincere about what he was saying and thinking. However, I wasn't! I was befuddled to think whether I was destined to drive the bullock carts only in my coming days. Then what use my being so brilliant in the arena of letters and numbers, that is, in academics? Nevertheless, I could not muster courage to tell my *Naanaajee* that day that I must needs not learn the skills to drive bullocks or bullock carts for earning a living or for completing the journey of my life.

On reaching home, too, my maternal grandfather conveyed this sad news to the family members that I did not know even how to drive a cart, and that my prospects were bleak as regards my future. Not only shelter, I was devoid of a future, too, as though!

XXX

38. Centre Topper & Vulgarism
Enter Protagonist

However slowly might the time be passing in childhood as well as young age, the year eventually was destined to pass; and pass it did. Our final exams – so-called Board Exams -- of 'Basic schools' were held at some other place that was quite afar; and it was only through the instrumentality of our beloved and affectionate teacher that we were taken there in his company; stayed there, too, overnight, and sat for exam the next day, all without an iota of discomfort. Or it may be that we did not have the faculty to feel unease or discomfort even in those rustic environs, where even bathing was to be done at the hand-pump in the open. The exam was a common exam where students of various schools had assembled. For the first time I felt that there might be other prodigy as well apart from me on this vast planet called Earth. Not only the entire Earth which is unimaginably vast, even in my catchment area there were multitudes of other children – students – who could be more intelligent than I was. I was taken aback, and also, felt somewhat overawed by this scenario at the Exam centre. There, every teacher was boasting of one's own students as being the most brilliant ones; there was no measure to decide as such as to who in fact was more intelligent. Every creature considered oneself as the most intelligent one.

Whether I stood first or not in the exam but my *Panditjee* declared that I had topped the Exam Centre; there was no wherewithal to verify this proclamation of our teacher. And now, at this distance in time, I feel that every teacher whoever was there conducting the tests for the kids of fifth grade would have declared in one's respective school that their particular student was the most brilliant one, and that he or she had topped the Exam Centre. Still my honour was salvaged by virtue of my affectionate teacher's wisdom and astuteness! I am thankful to him, by now the departed soul!

I relished the fame; fame of course I already had in my area and the family although. This was an additional feather in my cap. At every which forum my elders would exhibit me as the prodigy who had topped not only the school, but also, the Exam Centre. Topping the Exam Centre was considered to be a great feat indeed. Incidentally, later on, when after five more years, I passed my tenth grade Board exam, again I was declared the Centre topper by my school as well as teachers; whether true or false, I can't vouchsafe.

When I was enjoying my augmented glory and advertising in every alley of the village my spectacular feat, I was harbouring in my child's heart a notion that everybody whosoever would be glad to hear of it. However, it was not true. Whereas the social strata towards my *Naanaa*'s households celebrated my achievement, and also, propped me up, the urchins of those two backward dwellings at the edge of the village did not react favourably as per my expectations. The student who was studying in my class announced aloud at that moment that he had also stood first at the entire Centre. Nobody could have believed that claim of the urchin, I knew, but that sham claim of the boy marred my enthusiasm. I recollected my feats at my previous school and the envy of classmates that ensued in its wake, and was obliged to muse that 'no glory comes without its side effects, just as no beautiful blossom blooms without prickly thorns!'

Still, for my teacher had pronounced it, I kept on floating on the placid ocean of glory!

Nevertheless, when I reached the school for collecting the marksheet, my teacher prepared it by hand taking the help of scale and pencils and handed me a paper slip hardly 6"x4" on which were marked the scores I had made in various subjects. The marks were not very impressive, I felt. It was mentioned as 'Passed' but nowhere it was mentioned that I had stood first in the class or at the Centre. The same was the impression drawn by my father when he had a look at my mark-sheet when we reached our village after some time; even as, his feelings were reflected in his warped brows and distorted countenance while perusing my mark-sheet.

Incidentally, five years later, when I passed my High school exam and went to collect my mark-sheet, it was also handwritten only, of course, this time on a pre-printed format of mark-sheets, not on a plain paper ruled by hand. The handwriting of the person, the teacher, who wrote it was not as pretty as my marks were. Also, the ink on the not-so-good a paper or format had spilt. I did not feel good at that shoddy treatment of my marks. Good marks should have been written aesthetically, and on good paper, and also, in good handwriting, I had felt at that time. However, who cares for the sentiments of others or the feats of success of others, least of all those of hapless kids!

XXX

The End

English Books by *'Videh'*

Hypocrisy & Reality (fiction series: 9 books)

'Hypocrisy & Reality' is a fiction series comprising multiple books – novels. The fiction is aimed at depicting the hypocrisy of human society in every respect, be it the upbringing and treatment of babies, toddlers, children, adolescents, youths, or be it the treatment meted out to adults, aged ones, those who are closely related with oneself, with one's blood; not to speak of those called strangers or outsiders. Barring a rarity, nobody cares two hoots for the sentiments or security and safety of other living creatures on this sole planet nurturing 'living' beings!

Book 1: Beyond the Pale (fiction)

'Beyond the Pale' of Time & Space is the first volume of the long fiction series 'Hypocrisy & Reality' and as the name suggests, it deals with the timespan in the life of the protagonist when one had not even had a tryst with the concepts of Time and Space, nor did they make any difference in one's life if those ubiquitous phenomena were not taken cognizance of. Those were the years before the realm of schooling, the arena of perfect unconcern for the written letters, words, or numbers.

Book 2: Wilderness of Literacy (fiction)

'Wilderness of Literacy' is the second volume in the long fiction series 'Hypocrisy & Reality' and, as the name suggests, it takes the protagonist in the arena of letters, words, and numbers: the realm of what we call the 'literacy'. The experience of a child while treading this seemingly dreaded as well as untrodden landscape is nothing short of venturing into a wilderness; of course, led and mentored first by one's parents and thereafter invariably by their preceptors -- the masters -- all of whom have a tremendous amount of impact on the future human being that emerges from their inputs given and endeavours made towards making a man, the humanity.

Book 3: Advent of Time (fiction)

'Advent of Time' is the third volume in the long fiction series entitled 'Hypocrisy & Reality' and covers the schooling period when the protagonist discovered the phenomenon of Time, and also, figuratively he felt that it was then his time, even as, he mysteriously discovered his latent potential and wisdom catapulting himself into the uppermost orbits of glory, fame and all round applause from his classmates, masters as well as teachers. To his own amazement as well as bewilderment! Nevertheless, this providential blessing was not without its blemishes in the shape of rancour and envy of fellow classmates and their patrons towards him. Even as, Nature never allows anybody pleasure and praise without at the same time associating with them the equivalent amount of pain and back-biting!

Book 4: Devoid of Shelter (fiction)

'Devoid of Shelter', the fourth volume in the long fiction series 'Hypocrisy & Reality' furthers the journey of the protagonist into the world where he discovered to his dismay that he had no place on the globe which he could call as his home; he had no place of his own where he could take shelter during the day, and during the night. He somehow made do with seeking shelter with the relatives – maternal chiefly; not as a transitory phenomenon, but for good, until he himself took command of his life, snatching himself away from the indolent lifestyle of his parents. He also discovered during the refuge that however meritorious one might be, without the good base of ancestry, one was not considered as such.

Book 5: Price of Refuge (fiction)

'**Price of Refuge**', the fifth volume in the fiction series 'Hypocrisy & Reality' furthers the journey of the protagonist into the world when he returned to his paternal relatives and found to his dismay that his father was absolutely incapable of arranging a dwelling of his own. Also, he found himself to be a mute subject to child abuse at the hands of none other than supposedly an elder cousin of his, the son of his so-called benefactors who provided refuge in their vacant house. That was the price paid by the child for the indolence and handicaps of an unworthy father for seeking shelter under the tutelage of so-called relatives. No refuge seemingly looking innocuous goes without some price to be paid either by self, spouse or one's children.

Book 6: Hatred towards Love (fiction)

'**Hatred towards Love**', the sixth volume in the fiction series 'Hypocrisy & Reality' furthers the journey of the protagonist into the world where to his amusement he found himself catapulted into the realm of a celebrity or at least a child prodigy as far as the small rural catchment area was concerned. By virtue of his giftedness in the realm of

studies and his bewitching countenance, the classmates, especially, the lasses of her age could not help restraining themselves from loving him; and they did it overtly, without caring for the opinions and feelings of other class-fellows. Albeit the protagonist himself wallowed in the faulty ideology that having any truck with fair sex was anathema and a great sin which could not be washed away in later life.

Book 7: Towards the Yoga (fiction)

'**Towards the Yoga**', the seventh volume in the fiction series 'Hypocrisy & Reality' dwells on the period in the journey of life of the protagonist when he was at the pinnacle of his bodily prowess and psychic acuity, thanks to his habit of pursuing *Yogaasans* regularly as well as religiously. As though something divine was associated with the pursuit of *Yogaasans*, his father luckily could get an *ad hoc* teacher's job in the town school too; however, that was not to be sustained throughout for at the fag-end of the academic session, his father fell out with the Principal of school and was expelled. *Yoga,* nevertheless, gave the protagonist a hue that was unparallelled, and which materialised into the worldly as well as societal fame for him.

Book 8: On the Descent (fiction)

'**On the Descent**', the eighth volume in the fiction series 'Hypocrisy & Reality' takes the protagonist over the hump. He was then a ward of such a guardian who did not have any wherewithal to run his household, yet had no qualms about begetting more issues, more and more at that. Agriculture, of course, he had as an inheritance but he was by nature averse to anything even distantly associated with agriculture or Nature, for that matter. Any industrious as well as expedient agriculturalist would have eked out one's livelihood quite easily from the fifteen *beeghaa*s of arable land his father had inherited from his resourceful, brave as well as powerful ancestors, but not he.

Book 9: In the Exile (fiction)

'In the Exile', the ninth volume in the fiction series 'Hypocrisy & Reality' furthers the journey of the protagonist into the world where post his dramatic jump into the orbit of fame in the wake of his High School result, he found himself entirely in a barren land where he could see no ray of hope from his father, even as, the latter was totally incapable of arranging the means to further the studies for his exceptionally gifted son. For the first time, the protagonist realised that his father was incapable of meeting his requirements for pursuing further studies. He was already suffering emotionally having been separated from his mother for the first time! This was for him like an exile, that too, very uncomfortable!

Bewailing Muse (poetry)

Be it the sage *Valmeeki* or be it the modern poet *Sumitraa Nandan Pant*, both have held that poetry has its founts in heart and is the outcome of extreme sorrow, misery or pangs of separation. Poetry cannot be created; it gets engendered out of compulsion. From the heart! Heart's language is poetry or musing! I have offered to christen them as Muse: 'Bewailing Muse'; the first musings out of wailings! Nevertheless, I am tempted not to treat them as children's literature for I sense some

substantial element, too, in them. The period of the composition of these poems is from 1972 to 1976; and I feel that my wailings have not fallen on deaf ears, so to say, given my present circumstances of life which are totally opposite to the then prevailing ones!

Chambellion (drama: comedietta)

In the genre of Drama (Comedietta), here is the playlet 'Chambellion' that exposes the bizarre reality of the political developments post transfer of reins from the whites to the yellow people in the guise of 'Democracy' and 'Independence'; whereas actually the latter have been pursuing their dynastic agenda and propagating their own family fiefdoms that have flourished like weeds in multitudes in the void created by annihilation of Princely states and Landlords. Allegorically, it may be compared with the weed flourishing in an agricultural field which has remained unsown after harvest of the previous crop. For the subjects, verily, there is no Freedom whatsoever, in literal sense.

Brainy Beasts (short stories)

This is an anthology of short stories, included wherein are four short stories or farces, so to say, that is, anecdotes including the 'In An Illegible Script', which is the English version of the author's *Hindee* short story '*Anpadh Lipi Mein...* (अनपढ़ लिपि में)' that was first published in now extinct though the then prestigious *Hindee* magazine the 'Kaadambinee' way back in July, 1992, with quite an applause and accolades from the sides of kind readers! Other stories or anecdotes are also those published in other places, i.e. journals of variegated hues. Nothing uttered in these works is meaningless; this conviction is at work behind the inspiration to publish them in book form for kind readers.

Search for Life (translation of 'Hatyaaree Sadee Mein Jeevan Kee Khoj' (हत्यारी सदी में जीवन की खोज))
English Translation by *'Videh' Arvind Kumar* of *Hindee* poetry book *'Hatyaaree Sadee Mein Jeevan Kee Khoj' (हत्यारी सदी में जीवन की खोज)* by renowned young poet *'Nirvikaar' Mukesh Kumar*. This book has earned *'Nirvikaar'* the award of *'Jai Shankar Prasaad Puraskaar'* of Rs. One Lac from the *'Rajya Karmchaaree Saahitya Sansthaan, Uttar Pradesh'*. On the *Hindee* book *'Hatyaaree Sadee Mein Jeevan Kee Khoj,'* critiques by renowned personalities -- both young and old -- like *Ashwaghosh, Prempaal Sharmaa, Rajeev Saxena, Dr Anoop Singh, Dr Devkee Nandan Sharmaa, Manoj Kumaar Jhaa, Gautam Rajarshi,* etc have been published in various journals and magazines. The renowned critic Dr *Om Nishchal* has included this anthology in the select category for *'Kavya Paridrishya'* of 2017 amongst the famous poetry books.

Reality of Invisible (translation of 'Adrishya Kaa Yathaarth' (अदृश्य का यथार्थ))
English translation by *'Videh' Arvind Kumar* of the *Hindee* poetry book *'Adrishya Kaa Yathaarth' (अदृश्य का यथार्थ)* by renowned poet *'Ashwaghosh' Om Prakaash Sharmaa*. *'Ashwaghosh'* -- a well-known moniker of *Hindee* world! A litterateur of impeccable renown! Praised by multitudes -- both in literary and plebeian spheres! He has been composing prolifically -- having published over two dozen books spanning all the genre! The thesis, the short stories, the short epics, the anthologies, the new genre songs, the *ghazals*, the poetry for children *et al.* Covering all age groups! He has been honoured with many awards in literary and academic fields by prestigious institutions.

Nagasaki: Bomb & Aftermath (commentary on the first novel of Nobel Laureate, Kazuo Ishiguro) (Displayed on Oxford bookstore)
This is a work of literary study into the first novel 'The Pale View of Hills' by 2017 Literature Nobel Laureate, Kazuo Ishiguro, who has narrated in a mesmerising style of story telling the tale of Japanese society undergoing change in the aftermath of dropping of atomic bomb. The Americans not only vanquished and occupied the Japanese military and land by dropping the most lethal weapon never before heard of – the atomic bomb – on two of the Japanese cities, one of which was Nagasaki which witnessed this technological devastation on 8th of August, 1945, but also, occupied the minds and hearts of Japanese youth, both men and women. The youth of Japan started decrying everything old and conventional including their erstwhile education system and the ideologies of patriotism and nationalism.

Procreation, the Adorable (English summary of Shiv Puraan)

The *Shiva-ling* has ever been a matter of amazement and mystery for mankind. That something obscure is there behind the adoration of such a carnal symbol as *ling* irrespective of the same being that of a deity called *Shiva* has ever been lingering in my mind. Why should a large majority of population in this land – from north to south -- worship the genitals so openly, so brazenly? So reverently! *Shiva* is supposed to be a mythological persona, in existence too long back in time, who might have been the pioneer in realizing the spectacular qualities of *ling* and *yoni*, specifically, those of converting the *sthaavar* (the insensate) into *jangam* (the sensate) and those of creating the *satva-lok*, (conscious beings).

Self-Styled Sovereign, the Judiciary (Dramatic deliberation on the state of judiciary)

This is in fact an academic deliberation on the functioning and reality of the judicial system prevalent in India post what they euphemistically call the 'Independence' or, literally, the *'Aazaadee'*. Whose Independence was it anyway? For whom? Except for the ruling class? The lawyers first, and then the hooligans of *Chambal*. Nonetheless, the judiciary of the free country turned out to be one step further than its new crop of leaders; they usurped the entire authority from the latter in subtle moves one after the other. In olden epochs, the autocratic *Sultaans* or *Baadshaahs* dispensed justice purely depending upon their whims and fancies, which were incidental to the moods and tantrums of the Sovereign. Historically as well, the Real Sovereign was the one who dispensed justice. The Judiciary in Indian Republic soon realised this and acted.

XXX

'विदेह' रचित हिंदी ग्रंथ

अनपढ़ लिपि (कहानी-संग्रह)

'विदेह' अरविन्द कुमार की आठ हिंदी कहानियों का संकलन! संकलन की पहली कहानी 'अनपढ़ लिपि में ...' जुलाई, 1992 में प्रतिष्ठित हिंदी पत्रिका 'कादंबिनी' में छपी थी। 'सिग्नेचर' भी स्वच्छता के प्रति सरकारी महकमे की विद्रूपात्मक मनोदशा का कड़वा चित्रण है। 'ताकि आप अपने पक्ष में रहें!' नये प्रकार के कर्मचारियों की मानसिकता को इंगित करती है। फिर फिर वही लोग' भेड़-बकरियों की तरह दुरुपयोग किये जा रहे जन-समुदाय के विषय में कहानी है। 'अपार्थाइड': वस्तुतः तो, शक्तिशाली और निर्बल का भेद ही असली रंग-भेद है। नया वेद' 'आज़ादी' नाम से वही पारम्परिक पद्धति चतुराई-पूर्वक 'नया संविधान' के नाम से चलाये जाने की पोल-पट्टी खोलती है। 'पहली कमाई' कहानी का आख्यान कल्पना से भी अधिक विस्मयकारी है! 'भगवान को पैसा' समाज और सरकार दोनों ही की धन के प्रति जो दृष्टि है, उस पर तीखा व्यंग्य है।

पाषाण-युग (कहानी-संग्रह)

'विदेह' अरविन्द कुमार की सात हिंदी कहानियों का संकलन! संकलन की पहली कहानी 'ब्लॉक का पेड़' आज के समाज में क्षीण होते हुए आपसी सौहार्द्र, एवं अजनबियों के प्रति बढ़ते अकारण वैमनस्य, को बिंबित करती हुई सच्चाई है। मेरी

ज्ञाति' भारत में जातियों के हास्यास्पद 'प्रहसन' – फ़ार्स (farce) -- को चित्रित करके इसकी विद्रूपता को व्यंजित करती है। 'हिंदू-मुसलमान' साम्प्रदायिकता के प्रश्न को व्यक्तियों – दो घनिष्ठ मित्रों -- के स्तर पर परीक्षण करके देखती है। 'मुर्गबाज' समय की नब्ज पर हाथ रखने की कोशिश है। 'मंदिरों, मस्जिदों, गुरुद्वारों, गिरजाघरों में ...' साम्प्रदायिक कट्टरता की निरर्थकता को व्यंजित करने के लिए है, जो मृत्यु के पर्दे के पीछे कितनी हास्यास्पद बन जाती है! ऐ अधर्मी!' आदमी की नश्ल को बदलने की नाहक कोशिश कही जा सकती है। 'राक्षस' इस नये शासन-प्रशासन में व्याप्त भ्रष्टाचार पर एक व्यंग्यात्मक टिप्पणी है, और बताती है कि राक्षस कोई कपोल-कल्पना नहीं है, बल्कि आज भी एक वास्तविकता है।

निसर्ग (कहानी-संग्रह)

'विदेह' अरविन्द कुमार की सात हिंदी कहानियों का संकलन! संकलन की पहली कहानी 'मुलाक़ात एक बड़े लेखक से' एक बड़े लेखक और एक आम आदमी के जीवन के साम्य और अंतर दोनों को ही उजागर करती है। 'फाड़ी हुई कविता' एक ऐसे पति की व्यथा-कथा है, जो एक कवि एवं साहित्यकार भी है। 'नया साल' में कुछ भी नया नहीं होता, फिर भी सारी दुनिया किस कदर बाबली हुई रहती है। 'हितैषिणी' शादी जैसी संस्थाओं के पाखण्ड, फरेब एवं परम्पराओं से चिपकाव की विद्रूपता पर सशक्त प्रहार करती है। 'छोटे-से शरीर में कैदी' शिशुमन की विवशता को चित्रित करती है; वह पूरी तरह माँ-बाप की मूर्खताओं पर निर्भर रहने को विवश है। 'निसर्ग' एक रोमांटिक कहानी है। 'टूट-टूटकर गिरते सितारे' दिखाती है कि कैसे समाज अपने ही शिकंजे में फँसा रहकर ही परेशान होता रहता है!

आर्त-गान (कविता-संग्रह)

'वियोगी होगा पहला कवि, आह से उपजा होगा गान

उमड़कर आँखों से चुपचाप, बही होगी कविता अनजान!'

(सुमित्रा नंदन पंत)

या

'मा निषाद त्वम् गम: प्रतिष्ठाम् शाश्वती समा:
यत् क्रौंच मिथुनादेकम् त्वम् वधी: काम मोहितम्!'
(महर्षि वाल्मीकि)

चाहे तो आदि कवि वाल्मीकि हों, चाहे फिर छायावादी कवि पंत हों, एक बात तो तय है, कि कविता वियोग या विषाद या शोक से उत्सृजित होती है। पहले-पहल की रचनाएँ हैं ये – जीवन के पहले-प्रहर की; अतः बच्चों के उपयुक्त ही हो सकती हैं। बाल-कविता! बाल-कविता इसे मैंने फिर भी इसलिए नहीं कहा है, क्योंकि इनमें मुझे कुछ सार भी सन्निहित लगता रहा है; एकदम तो बकवास नहीं ही हैं ये, जैसी कि बाल (अबोध) -कविता की प्रकृति और प्रवृत्ति होती है। ये कविताएँ 1972 से 1976 के काल-खंड में सृजित हैं; और अभी लगभग अर्ध-शती की परिपक्व दृष्टि से भी परिमार्जित!

काल-क्रंदन (कविता-संग्रह)

जीवन के प्रथम प्रहर की हृदयाभिव्यक्तियों (1972 से 1976 तक) के 'आर्त-गान' के बाद, 1979 से 1990 तक के द्वादश वर्षीय काल-खण्ड में मैंने जो क्रंदन किया था, उसे मैने कविता कहा; और उन कविताओं का 'काल-रेख' नाम मैंने चुना था; क्योंकि काल की छाती पर 12 वर्षों तक मैं जो घिसटता रहा था, उस लकीर पीटने को 'काल-रेख' कहना ही मुझे रुच रहा था। परन्तु, कुछ काव्यात्मक स्फुरणा के वश, कुछ काल-अंतराल के प्रभाव-वश मैं अब इसे 'काल-क्रंदन' ही कहना अधिक समीचीन समझ रहा हूँ। साहित्य -- और इसीलिए कविता भी -- जीवन के मूल की अर्थात् सत्य की खोज है: सत्य की परख, यथार्थ की परख! इसमें सब कुछ सुनने-सुनाने, गाने-गवाने ही योग्य है, ऐसा दावा मैं नहीं करता। परन्तु, क्या पढ़ने-पढ़ाने योग्य है, और क्या नहीं, इसका निर्णय भी तो मैं नहीं कर सकता; क्योंकि इसका कण-कण मेरा नितांत निजी सच है! इसमें कितना किस और किसी का भी सच प्रस्तुत है, यह निर्णय उन्हीं पर!

अननुभूत काल (कविता-संग्रह)

अब यह तीसरी काव्य-पुस्तक है! एकदम नवीन काल से सम्बंधित! अभी-अभी हो गुज़रे बड़े मानवीय हादसे को रेखांकित करती हुई: कोरोना की महा-आपदा! विश्व-आपदा! जो न कभी हुई

थी, और आशा एवम् प्रार्थना ही कर सकते हैं, न कभी भविष्य में होगी! एकदम नये रूप में दुनिया को सोचने को मजबूर होना पड़ा: 'ऐसा भी हो सकता है?' बेतहाशा भागम-भाग में लगी दुनिया अचानक रुक-सी गयी; नहीं, रुक ही गयी – शब्दशः। वायुयान रुक गये, रेलयान रुक गये, बसें रुक गयीं, सारे वाहन रुक गये। मंदिर, मस्जिद, गुरुद्वारे और चर्च भी बंद हो गये: परमात्मा के घर थे वे! हैं! मक्का, मदीना बंद हो गये। वेटिकन बंद हो गया। वह चिरंतन अटूट आस्था जो रुकने का नाम नहीं लेती थी, और आए-दिन छोटी-छोटी बातों पर सिर-फुटव्वल को बेताब रहती थी, अचानक अपने को सकपकाता हुआ पाने लगी। क्या वह बस आस्था ही भर थी, दुनियाबी प्राणियों को भरमाने के लिए; क्या उसमें कोई पारमार्थिक सार न था? तार्किक मन यह सोचने को विवश हो गया। इस कोरोना-काल ने बहुत सारे पाखण्ड-मण्डन किये हैं!

अम्बेडकर-स्मृति (नाटिका)

जाति की समस्या भारत देश के लिए भयंकर होती जा रही है। यह जाति ही है जिसके चलते भारत-भूमि आक्रांताओं के समक्ष प्रणत हो गयी थी। कड़वी सच्चाई यह है कि राजनीतिक चतुराई के चलते 'सत्ताधीशों' ने अपने आप को 'ऊँचा' और सत्ता से 'वंचित' जनों को 'नीचा' मानना शुरू कर दिया। 'आज़ादी' के अधकचरे प्रयोग के चलते स्थिति और भी भयावह हो गयी है; 'नीचे लोग' ऊँचे लोगों को गरियाते रहते हैं: उसके लिए वे 'मनु-स्मृति' नाम की किसी पौराणिक पुस्तक को गरियाते रहते हैं, जबकि वास्तविकता यह है कि आधुनिक भारत के 99.99 प्रतिशत लोगों ने उस पुस्तक का पढ़ना तो दूर, नाम तक नहीं सुना है। उधर, नये सत्ताधीशों ने नयी स्मृति लिखकर -- संविधान लिखकर (जिसकी ड्राफ्टिंग समिति के अध्यक्ष होने के नाते अम्बेडकर को श्रेय मिला हुआ है) – पूर्ववर्ती समाज-व्यवस्था एवं अर्थ-व्यवस्था को एक सिरे से नकार और नेस्तनाबूद कर दिया है। समाज के बीच इस पर जो बहस चल रही है, उसी का एक छोटा सा नमूना है यह एकांकी!

प्रिय-प्रवास (संकलन, 'हरिऔध' के महाकाव्य का)

'प्रिय-प्रवास' हिंदी -- खड़ी बोली -- का प्रथम महाकाव्य है, जो स्वनाम धन्य महाकवि अयोध्या सिंह उपाध्याय 'हरिऔध' की अमर कृति है। अत्यंत सुमधुर काव्य के रूप में युग-पुरुष श्रीकृष्ण के गोकुल से मथुरा प्रवास और उनके वियोग से व्यथित गोकुल-वासियों की विरह-वेदना का सरस चित्रण इसमें है। वह एक प्रकार से हर प्राणी की वेदना ही है, जो वह उस समय अनुभव करता है जब कोई स्वजन प्रवास हेतु जाता है या प्रयाण करता है, जो कि संसृति का अपरिहार्य लक्षण ही है। आसक्ति, मोह और ममता सब दुःखों का मूल है; जबकि ज्ञान दुःखों से मुक्ति का साधन! इस महा-आख्यान का यही सार अथच् केंद्रीय संदेश समझ में आता है! 'प्रिय-प्रवास' विरह, बिछुड़ने की वेदना, नैसर्गिक प्रेम और विश्व-कल्याण के संदेश का ही महाकाव्यात्मक सरस रूप है। 'विदेह' अरविन्द कुमार ने इस अद्भुत साहित्यिक कृति को पुनर्संकलित एवं पुनर्मुद्रित करके इसकी एक संक्षिप्त गद्य-कथा भी इसमें प्रस्तुत की है।

प्रार्थना एवं प्राणांश (संकलित प्रेरक काव्यांश)

बहुत ही सरस और सार्थक प्रार्थनाओं एवं प्रेरणादायी काव्यांशों का संचयन है यह! जो न जाने कहाँ-कहाँ से 'विदेह' अरबिंद कुमार ने अपनी रुचि अनुकूल संकलित एवं सम्पादित किया है, उन सभी मनीषियों के प्रति हार्दिक आभार व्यक्त करते हुए, जिनकी रचनाएँ और रचनाओं के प्राणांश इसमें संकलित किये गये हैं। जीवन, मृत्यु के वाहन के आगमन की प्रतीक्षा में रत यात्री के कार्य-कलाप और मनोदशा के अतिरिक्त और क्या है! इस प्रतीक्षा में क्या-क्या अनहोनी अनुभूतियाँ नहीं होतीं! इस प्रतीक्षा को कम कष्टकर करने के लिए काव्य-शास्त्र अनुश्रवण की अनुशंसा मनीषियों ने की है। साथ ही, प्रार्थना के माहात्म्य को भी स्वीकारा है।

'मनो पुब्बंगमा धम्मा, मनो सेट्ठा मनोमया!'

भगवान बुद्ध ने मन से ही सृजित होता हुआ इस सकल प्रपञ्च को बताया है। अत: मन को शुचि एवं निष्कंप रखकर आप संसार का अनुभव बदल सकते हैं। जब सभी कुछ कल्पित है, तो सबको अपना मत अनुभव जैसा ही लगता है। परन्तु, है वस्तुतः सब कुछ कपोल-कल्पित ही: न इसे सत्य कहने का कोई तात्पर्य है, न असत्य कहने का! बस मन को साधने का साधनभर है प्रार्थना!

महामुनि वाल्मीकि रचित् इतिहास :
उत्तरकाण्ड (वाल्मीकि के उत्तरकाण्ड का गद्यांतरित सारांश)

'रामायण' आदिकाव्य है, न केवल भारतवर्ष का, अपितु सकल मानव-समाज का भी। महर्षि वाल्मीकि-कृत यह काव्य-पुस्तक वस्तुतः तत्कालीन इतिहास है: उस राजवंश का, जिसकी कीर्ति हज़ारों वर्ष पश्चात् भी आज तक अक्षुण्ण है। उस राजवंश के तत्कालीन यशस्वी सम्राट 'राम' का इसमें वर्णन है। राम-राज्य की व्यवस्था, जिसका वर्णन ऋषि ने किया है, आज भी शासन-व्यवस्था के हेतु आदर्श मानी जाती है।

लेखक ने संस्कृत के ग्रंथ का मात्र सार रूप यहाँ प्रस्तुत किया है; सब प्रकार की काव्यात्मकता और अतिशयोक्तियों का निवारण करते हुए। साथ ही, आलंकारिकता को आधुनिक संदर्भों से जोड़ते हुए ऐतिहासिक-वैज्ञानिक अर्थों में भी विषय को समझाने का प्रयास किया है।

कितना यह किसको भाता है, यह तो हर व्यक्ति की अपनी-अपनी रुचि और सोच पर निर्भर करेगा; बहरहाल, लेखक ने अपना दृष्टिकोण प्रस्तुत किया है, वह भी इस चिन्ता से कि नयी पीढ़ी अपनी बहुमूल्य विरासत – गौरवशाली इतिहास -- की ओर एकदम ध्यान नहीं दे रही है। उसका एक कारण ग्रंथों का संस्कृत में होना, और दूसरा अत्यधिक प्रतीकात्मक होने के कारण कपोल-कल्पित-सा लगना, भी हो सकता है; उसी कारण का निवारण करने का यह विनीत प्रयास है।

XXX

लेखक-परिचय

'विदेह' अरविन्द कुमार

भारतीय साहित्य की उदात्त पीठिका को आधुनिक संदर्भों से संपृक्त करने वाले सारस्वत साधक एवं विशिष्ट लेखन-शैली के प्रणेता वरिष्ठ साहित्यकार श्री अरविन्द कुमार 'विदेह' का जन्म 6 अप्रैल 1957 ई को उत्तर प्रदेश के गौतमबुद्धनगर जनपद की जेवर तहसील के छोटे-से गाँव 'मारहरा' में हुआ था। आपके माता-पिता की मानव-मूल्यों में गहरी आस्था रही है। सीमित संसाधनों, बल्कि विपन्नता, के बावजूद भी आप सफलता के लाभी हुए। आपने तत्कालीन आगरा विश्वविद्यालय के अलीगढ़ स्थित धर्मसमाज कॉलेज से भौतिक विज्ञान में स्नातकोत्तर उपाधि प्राप्त की है। आप देश के प्रतिष्ठित बैंक – भारतीय स्टेट बैंक – में दीर्घकालीन सेवा प्रदान करने के उपरांत दिसम्बर, 2018 में सहायक महाप्रबंधक के पद से सेवा निवृत्त हुए हैं।

श्री 'विदेह' छात्र-जीवन से ही अत्यंत मेधावी रहे हैं। विज्ञान-संवर्ग के विद्यार्थी होते हुए भी आपकी साहित्य के प्रति गहरी अभिरुचि रही है। साहित्य के प्रति आपका अनुराग इतना प्रबल रहा है कि बैंकिंग सेक्टर में अति व्यस्त जीवन-शैली वाली नौकरी करते हुए भी आप साहित्य और लेखन से अनवरत रूप से जुड़े रहे हैं। उनकी रचनाएँ तत्कालीन 'कादम्बिनी' जैसी लब्ध-प्रतिष्ठ पत्रिकाओं में काफ़ी पहले छप चुकी हैं; और उनके अन्य लेख एवं कविताएँ अन्य हिंदी, अंग्रेज़ी पत्र-पत्रिकाओं में यदा-कदा छपते रहे हैं। साथ ही, आपने हिंदी एवं अंग्रेजी भाषा के साहित्य का विशद अध्ययन एवं सृजन किया है। संस्कृत एवं पाली भाषा के साहित्य में भी आपकी गहरी अभिरुचि है।

विभिन्न विधाओं में आपने अब तक 27 ग्रंथों का प्रणयन किया है, जिनमें 17 अंग्रेजी एवं 10 हिंदी भाषा में हैं। हिंदी की पुस्तकों में 03 कहानी-संग्रह (अनपढ़ लिपि, पाषाण युग, निसर्ग); 03 कविता-संग्रह (आर्त-गान, काल-क्रन्दन, अननुभूत काल); 01 नाटिका (अम्बेडकर-स्मृति); 01 काव्य-संचयन (प्रार्थना एवं प्राणांश) उल्लेखनीय हैं। इसके अतिरिक्त आपने खड़ी बोली के प्रथम महाकाव्य 'प्रिय-प्रवास' को भी पुनर्संकलित एवं पुनर्मुद्रित किया है; तथा साथ ही,

वाल्मीकि रामायण के उत्तरकाण्ड का गद्यांतरण इतिहास के दृष्टिकोण से आपने 'महामुनि वाल्मीकि रचित् इतिहास: रामायण – उत्तरकाण्ड' नामक पुस्तक के रूप में किया है।

अंग्रेजी भाषा में आपकी उपन्यास शृंखला 'Hypocrisy & Reality' है जिसके अब तक 9 खण्ड वह प्रस्तुत कर चुके हैं (Beyond the Pale; Wilderness of Literacy; Advent of Time; Devoid of Shelter; Price of Refuge; Hatred towards Love; Towards the *Yoga*; On the Descent; In the Exile)। इसके अतिरिक्त, 01 Comedietta (*Chambellion*); 01 Short Story collection (Brainy Beasts); 01 Poetry anthology (Bewailing Muse); 01 Drama (Self-styled Sovereign, the Judiciary); पौराणिक ग्रंथ 'शिव-पुराण' के आधुनिक संदर्भों में अध्ययन पर आधारित 01 पुस्तक (Procreation, the Adorable); 2017 के साहित्य नोबेल पुरस्कार विजेता, Kazuo Ishiguro, के प्रथम उपन्यास 'A Pale View of the Hills' पर आधारित 01 समीक्षात्मक ग्रंथ (Nagasaki: Bomb & Aftermath) हैं।

'विदेह' जितने मौलिक सर्जक हैं उतने ही समर्थ अनुवादक भी हैं। उन्होंने हिंदी के 02 काव्य-संग्रहों – 'निर्विकार' मुकेश के 'हत्यारी सदी में जीवन की खोज', और 'अश्वघोष' ओमप्रकाश शर्मा के 'अदृश्य का यथार्थ' – का काव्यात्मक अनुवाद अंग्रेजी में किया है, जो क्रमश: 'Search for Life' एवं 'Reality of Invisible' के नाम से प्रकाशित हुई हैं।

'विदेह' के व्यक्तित्व का निर्माण घोर विपन्नता और कठोर संघर्षों ने किया है, जिसका प्रभाव उनकी लेखन-शैली पर निर्भीक अभिव्यक्ति और बेबाकी के रूप में देखा जा सकता है। आपके जीवन का अनुभव अत्यन्त व्यापक रहा है। आपने विपन्नता भी भोगी है, और सुख-सुविधा-सम्पन्न अमेरिकी जीवन भी जीया है; साथ ही, अनेक विदेश-यात्राओं का भी आपको अनुभव है।

केवल साहित्य ही नहीं, 'विदेह' की प्रवृत्तियों में ध्यान-साधना, विपश्यना, योग-साधना, प्राकृतिक-जीवन, आरोग्य, शाकाहार, बागवानी, पर्यटन और पैदल भ्रमण भी सम्मिलित हैं।

2024 के हिंदी दिवस पर – 14 सितंबर को – 'विदेह' को 'शुभम् साहित्य, कला एवम् संस्कृति संस्थान' द्वारा उनके सर्वोच्च सम्मान 'शुभम् रत्न' से सम्मानित किया गया।

'विदेह' की पुस्तकें 'Notion Press', Blue Rose One, Amazon और Flipkart पर तीनों ही प्रारूपों – ebooks, paperback एवम् hard cover – में उपलब्ध हैं।

XXX

About the Author

'Videh' Arvind Kumar

An unflinching adorer of the goddess of wisdom, the *Saraswatee*, and the one who has associated the lofty traditions of Indian literature with the present day contexts, and also, an author of an uncanny style of his own, the seasoned litterateur, *'Videh' Arvind Kumar*, was born on 6th of April, 1957, at a hamlet called *'Maar-Haraa'* in *Jewar Tehseel* of *Gautam Buddha Nagar* distt. in UP. His parents were staunch votaries of human values. Despite unbearable financial constraints, rather extreme wretchedness, he overcame the hurdles of existence and succeeded. He is a post-graduate in Physics from D S College, *Aleegarh*, affiliated to the then *Aagaraa* University. He retired as an Asstt General Manager from the esteemed Bank – State Bank of India – after putting in a long as well as illustrious service there.

'Videh' has been meritorious ever since his school days. Despite being a science stream scholar, he has been showing a keen interest in literature all along. His bonding with literature has been so strong that notwithstanding his pursuing such a busy job as Banking, he managed to sustain his love for literature. His works have been published decades back in the then esteemed magazines such as 'Kaadambinee'. Also, his stray articles and compositions have found place in various magazines and journals now and then. Besides, he has been a voracious reader of literature and other stuff both in *Hindee* and English languages, apart from himself being a prolific writer and a poet. He is also an adorer of the literature in *Sanskrit* and *Pali* languages.

In variegated genre he has composed as many as 27 books so far, of which, 17 are in English and 10 in *Hindee*. Among the *Hindee* books, there are 03 story anthologies (*Anapadh Lipi; Paashaan Yug; Nisarg*); 03 poetry anthologies (*Aaart Gaan; Kaal Krandan; Ananubhoot Kaal*); 01 drama (*Ambedkar Smriti*); 01 collection of select poetic pieces (*Praarthanaa evam Praanaansh)*. Aside of this, he has compiled, commented, edited and got re-published the first epic of the *Khadee Bolee Hindee*, the *Priya Pravaas*; and a book entitled *'Mahaamuni Vaalmeeki Rachit Itihaas: Raamaayan -- Uttar Kaand'* which presents, in succinct prose form, the ancient history of India as narrated in the most ancient epic.

As regards English oeuvre of '*Videh*', he has so far published 9 volumes of the long fiction series 'Hypocrisy & Reality' (Beyond the Pale; Wilderness of Literacy; Advent of Time; Devoid of Shelter; Price of Refuge; Hatred towards Love; Towards the *Yoga*; On the Descent; In the Exile) with yet more planned to come. Besides, 01 Comedietta (*Chambellion*); 01 Short Story collection (Brainy Beasts); 01 Poetry anthology (Bewailing Muse); 01 Drama (Self-Styled Sovereign, the Judiciary); 01 book based on the study of mythological volume '*Shiva Puraan*' in the present day context (Procreation, the Adorable); 01 commentary book on the first novel – 'A Pale View of the Hills' -- of the 2017 Nobel Literature laureate, Kazuo Ishiguro (Nagasaki: Bomb & Aftermath) are other books.

Not only an original writer as well as thinker, but also, a capable and versatile translator is '*Videh*' inasmuch as he has translated in English free verse form 02 *Hindee* poetry anthologies, viz. '*Hatyaaree Sadee Mein Jeevan Kee Khoj*' of '*Nirvikaar*' *Mukesh Kumaar,* and '*Adrishya Kaa Yathaarth*' of '*Ashwaghosh*' *Omprakaash Sharmaa* with the titles of the books being *seriatim* as 'Search for Life' and 'Reality of Invisible'.

The persona of '*Videh*' has been moulded by constant struggles and abject adversities, which have metamorphosed into his style of narration being quite frank as well as bland, if only straightforward.

His experiences of life are multifarious. He has not only suffered the pangs of extreme poverty and adversity in his childhood, but also, enjoyed the comforts and pleasures of the modern world by living in America.

Besides, he has visited and toured in various foreign countries, too.

Not only in literature, but also, in exotic pursuits like meditation, spiritual practice, *Vipashyanaa, Yoga* practice, naturopathy, natural living, *Aarogya,* vegetarianism, gardening, tourism and long walks on foot *'Videh'* is equally active.

To add to his laurels, *'Videh'* has been honoured with their highest honour *'Shubham Ratna'* by the institution *'Shubham Saahitya, Kalaa Evam Sanskriti Sansthaan'* on the occasion of *Hindee Divas*, i.e. on 14th September, 2024.

The books of *'Videh'* are available in all the three formats, viz. eBooks, paperbacks and hardcovers from the Notion Press, Blue Rose One, Amazon and the Flipkart.

XXX

Table of Contents